PETE'S DISAPPEARING ACT

JENNY TRIPP

PETE'S DISAPPEARING ACT

*** With illustrations by JOHN MANDERS ***

HARCOURT CHILDREN'S BOOKS
HOUGHTON MIFFLIN HARCOURT
Boston ★ New York ★ 2009

Harcourt Children's Books is an imprint of
Houghton Mifflin Harcourt Publishing Company.

www.hmhbooks.com

Library of Congress Cataloging-in-Publication Data
Tripp, Jenny.
Pete's disappearing act / Jenny Tripp ; with illustrations by John Manders.—1st ed.
p.   cm.
Summary: When Pete the performing poodle and Rita the chimp are
swept away from the circus in a tornado, they encounter frightening
adventures—and make new friends—as they try to return home.
[1. Poodles—Fiction. 2. Dogs—Fiction. 3. Adventure and adventurers—Fiction.
4. Voyages and travels—Fiction.] I. Manders, John, ill. II. Title.
PZ7.T73572Pf 2009
[Fic]—dc22
2008027525
ISBN 978-0-15-206177-7

Text set in New Astor
Book design by April Ward

First edition
A   C   E   G   H   F   D   B

Manufactured in the United States of America

For Ms. Kitty and Pooch,
whose showstopping stunts and
astonishing exploits never cease
to amaze their adoring mom

—J.T.

* * ⭐ * *

Time is a circus, always packing
up and moving away.

—BEN HECHT,
one of Hollywood and Broadway's
greatest writers

CHAPTER 1

FIRST OFF, I SWEAR to tell the truth and nothing but. Even the parts that make me look like a mutt. Before I begin, you've gotta understand two things.

The first is me.

Poodles don't usually come in pink. But I'm not your usual poodle. I'm a pure breed. Royal standard.

Pierre Le Chien's the name. You can call me Pete. Circus Martinez is my home, and Moliere's Performing Pups are my troupe. Showbiz is my pedigree. I'm not just in the circus, pal. I *am* circus.

And it's the same with my fellow performers, from the high-stepping Lipizzaner mares to the smallest chick in Senora Paloma's bird act. For nine months a year, our home is the open road. Our living room is a big striped tent and our bedrooms are railroad cars. It's a rough-and-tumble life. But if you were to offer me to trade it for a silken pillow and a palace full of porterhouses, I'd roll over laughing. Me, leave the circus? Never!

The other thing you've got to understand is Rita. Rita's our chimp. I like her about as much as I like fleas. Rita's always felt the same about me. So, when my old partner quit showbiz, she was the last animal I expected to ask me to start a new act.

But the more I chewed on the idea, the better I liked it. Sure, her sense of humor was foul. Her personal hygiene was worse. And her laugh could shatter glass. But when it came to work, she was a real pro. And it wasn't like I had any better offers.

It worked out fine—at first. I did all the highly skilled stuff, of course. Dancing on the rolla-bolla ball, twirling the tasseled baton in my teeth. Rita clowned it up, riding the little bike around the ring and pulling funny faces. She'd toss me balls, and I'd bounce them off my nose right back at her. The audience ate it up. And in no time the ringmaster had moved "Pete and Rita" up to the prime spot at the end of the first act. Everything was peachy keen.

Until Rita got bored.

Or was it jealous? Whatever it was, it reared its ugly head after rehearsal one day.

"Why do I have to stand around like a rube, while you do your little tra-la-la on the ball?" Rita asked, picking at her orange.

I blinked, surprised. "Because, Rita, the rolla-bolla ball is *my* star turn. If you're juggling or whatever at the same time, you're gonna confuse the audience. See?"

Rita scowled. "Why do you get a star turn? All I get is the crummy bike. Why can't I do some tightrope walking or . . ."

"The name of the act is 'Pete and Rita.' Me on top. Nobody gives top billing to a chimp."

I caught an evil glint in her eye. "Oh, really? And why is that?"

I sighed. "Three little words. Man's best friend. That's me."

Her rubbery lips sneered. "You're saying I can't be their best friend, too?"

"You're more like an oddball cousin."

Rita pitched the orange at me. Despite my lightning-fast reflexes, it popped me in the ear. My head rang like a gong.

"What's the big idea?" I snarled.

"You're afraid I'll be the star!" Rita spat right back.

Pathetic, huh? I shook my head. "Face it, Rita. Some of us are born to be top banana. Some of us are lucky to get any bananas at all."

Her little eyes narrowed. She leaned so close to my face that I thought she might bite me. "We'll see about that!" she said and went barreling out of the tent.

This testy exchange was watched by some of my fellow Performing Pups. Scrappy, the little comic mutt with the patch on one eye, shot me a worried look.

"Gosh, Pete, that was harsh."

Huh? What had I done, except tell the truth? Rita was the one throwing things! But the rest of the dogs were giving me the fish eye, too, from Lolly the pup to the big shaggy wolfhound, Arthur.

"Hey, she started it!" I whined. "You all saw that."

Bob, the white poodle, shook his head. "Hard to say who started it. But if I know Rita, she'll finish it."

How right he was. Our big finish was coming the very next night.

CHAPTER 2

IT WAS A SWELTERING Saturday in September. Our tour was almost over. In a couple of weeks, we'd be headed to Florida for our hard-earned winter break. There'd be plenty of chow and long naps. All of us animals looked forward to it. Rest and relaxation!

But tonight was showtime. I hadn't seen Rita since she'd gone off in a huff. She was waiting in the wings just like nothing had happened. When the band struck up our music, I jumped up behind her on the bike, put my paws on her shoulders, and barked, "Let's go!"

A spotlight found us as we came whizzing out of the wings. The audience broke into cheers. Our costume lady had made us a pair of matching silver vests, with a spangled skirt for Rita. As we flew around the ring, I could see sparkles dancing on the tent.

Rita skidded to a stop front and center and we jumped off. I hopped around on my hind legs to the music. Rita jigged and flapped her skirt. Funny stuff. The kids in the bleachers howled with delight. Then, out of nowhere, Rita grabbed me by the forepaws and started waltzing me around!

Youch!

"What are you trying to do," I snarled under my breath, "pull 'em off?" Rita grinned her toothy grin and let go.

"Ah, keep your shirt on," she hissed. "I'm just trying to freshen things up."

"Stick with the act!" I snapped.

The next bit was the jump rope. Rita picked up a length of silvery cord tied to the center pole and started twirling it. I jumped in on cue, hopping to the music.

Big applause, like always.

Now it was Rita's turn. I grabbed the rope in my jaws. But she went backflipping around the ring instead!

Disgusted, I spat out the rope. "Hey, Rita!" I barked. "Mind telling me what you're doing?"

"My new act," she hollered back. "I think I'll call it 'Rita and Pete.'"

Had she gone nuts?! I was so nervous I was panting. Rita was totally trashing our routine. What was I supposed to do? Roll over and let her steal the show? I could hear the ghosts of generations of Le Chiens barking at me, "Never!"

This was war.

I pranced over to the prop box, grabbed a rubber ball in my teeth, and tossed it in the air. I followed it with a second ball. Up on hind legs, I caught the first in my teeth, and tossed it high. Just in time, the next one came down, and I caught it and tossed it. Juggling's a cinch, if you've got hands. Try it with your teeth.

I could feel the eyes of the crowd turning to me. I picked up the pace, hopping around the ring as I tossed and caught in time to the music. A burst of applause told me I had the audience back where I wanted 'em.

Ha! Take that, you scene-stealing simian!

Suddenly, I heard laughter. Huh? I stole a glance at Rita.

There she stood, mugging, pretending to smother a huge yawn. Then she acted like she was checking her wristwatch. The audience roared.

I steamed. Pierre Le Chien is nobody's straight man—or dog. No way was I gonna play the chump for the chimp.

Now Rita was leaning against the center pole, pretending to be asleep and snoring. From where I was standing, I had a view of her furry rump.

How could I resist? I didn't even try.

I darted at her and—*sssnap!*—took a chomp.

That woke her up.

"Why, you four-footed flea circus!" she chittered. Then with a shriek that stabbed at my ears, Rita sprang at me. I ran for my life.

Now, in case you think I'd turned chicken, let me clue you in about chimps. First of all, they have arms like a circus strongman. Those fingers can do a lot of damage, particularly when they're wrapped around your throat. Second, chimps have big bad tempers. I knew Rita would be sorry after she'd choked me to death. But that wouldn't help me any. So I made like the wind and blew. Rita was hot on my heels, gibbering and screeching at the top of her lungs.

As we rounded the ring, she grabbed up the balls I'd been juggling and pitched them at me, hard. One bounced off my back and I stumbled, nearly going down in the sawdust. I could feel Rita's bony fingers sink into my curly pink fur!

Yip! I pulled free and dashed up the bleachers into the audience. Rita was pounding along right behind me. The audience thought it was all part of the show! But the band knew better. They swung into "Stars and Stripes Forever," which is circus code for *"HELP!"*

That brought the ringmaster running out into the ring. Spotting him, I tore down the opposite stairs, desperate and winded. He just stood there, jaw dropped. If he was holding me, I knew Rita wouldn't dare attack. All I had to do was get into his arms!

I made a leap at him. He stuck his hands out to block me. I tried to put on the brakes, but too late.

So I made a grab at his arm.

With my teeth.

Okay, I bit him! But I didn't mean to!

For an awful moment, I hung on him like a hornet's nest. Then the ringmaster hit the floor, me on top of him. *Boom!* Rita slammed into us like a screeching sack of cement. I scrambled to get under the ringmaster, who was screeching, too.

My trainer, Mike, came running out of the wings

with a couple of trapeze artists from the Flying Fuffer-nickles. They tossed a net over Rita and hustled her away.

Then Mike grabbed me by the collar—the collar!—and dragged me off. "Bad dog!" he scolded, half choking me with his iron grip.

Bad dog?! My nose burned with shame. And for what? An accidental dental encounter? A teensy little bite that hardly even broke the skin? I was the victim here. *Me!*

Well, wasn't I?

The circus world is pretty easygoing most ways. But even we have rules. I'd attacked my partner, and that's a big no-no. And I'd done it in front of an audience. Double no-no.

Worst yet, I'd bitten the ringmaster. Thereby breaking the most important rule of all, which is—

Never. Hurt. The. Humans.

Ever.

Because that can be fatal. For the animal, I mean.

Mike took me outside and chewed me out good. My tail was so far under me, I thought it might be gone forever. I tried giving him the ol' puppy-dog eyes, but

Mike wasn't buying it. He sent me to my basket, with out supper.

When the other dogs filed in after the show, I pretended to be asleep. I knew everyone was mad at me. I figured they'd cool down by tomorrow.

But I wasn't expecting the Ice Age.

CHAPTER 3

BY CHOW TIME the next morning, there was a definite chill in the air.

"'Morning, guys!" I yipped, trying to sound chipper. Nobody answered. Nobody even looked up.

The big cats had finished their morning meat. Zamba, our tiger, was scratching his back against the tent pole. He stopped to give me a dirty look. Lucky, the lion, was hunting a spot for a nap. Imelda Lipizzaner and her sisters, Sophie and Czarina, had their snoots stuck into their oat barrels. Rita was lounging on a trapeze, delicately skinning a banana with her feet. The Performing Pups were hitting the kibble. I started over to join them . . .

. . . and stopped.

Where was my bowl?!

Then I spotted it. Off in a lonesome corner, all by it-self. Where somebody had shoved it! So that's how it's gonna be. Bristling, I stalked to my breakfast. Or what should have been my breakfast. There weren't more than a couple of mouthfuls left.

"Hey!" I snarled. "Which one of you mutts had his muzzle in my meal?"

For a moment, everyone lifted their heads and looked at each other. Finally, Arthur, the wolfhound, spoke.

"Half rations today. For everybody."

Then they all went back to eating. My ears flattened in shame. Yikes! No wonder I was in the doghouse. I turned my back to them all. I didn't want to see their accusing looks. I gulped down the smidgen of chow in my bowl, determined not to hang around any longer than I had to.

As I was giving the bowl a last lick, I heard the thud and shuffle of hooves coming toward me. I looked over my shoulder to see the Lipizzaner sisters. The rest of the animals were gathering behind them. There was Rita, peeking out from behind Imelda's rump. Acting like she was scared of me. Ha!

Imelda didn't waste any time. Glaring down her

aristocratic prow at me, she whinnied, "Vhell, Peter? Vhat do you have to zhay for yourzhelf?"

Couldn't they see I felt crummy enough already for my part? "It was an accident! You know I didn't mean to bite the ringmaster!"

Her sister Sophie jumped in. "Accidents like zhat make circus look bad."

"And I'm still hungry!" Zamba rumbled.

Rita piped up. "Well, what about me? That was no accident!" I could hear the rest of the animals murmur agreement.

Why were they all taking her side? "It was Rita's fault!" I whined. "She started it."

Rita was doing her best to look pathetic, rubbing her behind and wincing. I noticed she was avoiding my eye.

Lolly took my side. "It *was* wrong of Rita to change the routine without telling Pete."

Rita abandoned the injured bit. "I tried! But he wouldn't listen. I just wanted to show him . . ."

"Yeah—show me up!" I snapped.

"I can do that without trying!" Rita spat back.

Grrr! I could feel my hackles rise.

But she wasn't finished. "I only joined up with you because I felt sorry for you!"

I was so mad, I was frothing at the mouth. "That's a low blow. Even for you, Banana Breath!" I stepped up to Rita and shoved my muzzle in her flat face. "I'm top dog in this outfit, and I'm gonna stay top dog. You don't like it? Tough! Find another partner!"

"Peter, vhat you are saying?" Sophie Lipizzaner neighed. "You and Rita are good togezzer."

"Yeah," Zamba agreed. "Everybody needs a partner. Look at me and Lucky." Lucky, now dozing on the floor, flicked his tail in agreement.

"Family sticks together. And we're all family here, Pete," Scrappy put in.

I shook my head until my ears flapped. "I don't know about you, Scraps, but there aren't any monkeys in my family tree."

I turned to my fellow canines. "What about you

guys? Are you gonna let this hairy-handed scene stealer get away with this?"

Arthur let me have it straight. "Pete, nobody likes a biter."

A biter?! "Oh, come off it, Artie! One little slip—" I whined.

"One? Ha!" There was Rita again. "What about the time on the train when you bit me on the ankle? I've still got the scar!"

PeeWee the ostrich had to stick his big beak in. "You snapped at me once, too! Just for talking!"

"You talk too much!" This was turning into a dog pile, with me on the bottom.

Imelda snorted. "Vhill you apologize to Rita?"

"Not until she apologizes to me!" I growled.

A silence stretched. They all looked at me. Then they all looked away. All of a sudden, it was like I wasn't even there anymore.

They were giving me the Silent Treatment.

My mind reeled. Not that!

The Silent Treatment is the worst penalty us circus animals can dish out to each other. I'd only seen it once before. Marvo the Mathematical Pony kicked a dog for messing up his entrance one night and got the Silent Treatment. It made him so miserable, he couldn't keep his figures straight. His trainer had to sell him to a riding stable.

The circus was my family, my world. Getting the Silent Treatment meant that, as far as the circus was concerned, Pete the Poodle was invisible. A ghost. A cold shudder ran down my backbone. Could I change their minds?

But Imelda and her sisters were already walking away. So were Zamba and PeeWee. Even Lucky, still snoring, rolled over. Desperate, I turned to the dogs.

"Guys, hey! Come on! We're a pack! Don't listen to them!"

Too late. Lolly sent me a last heartbroken glance, then joined the rest.

Traitors! Well, I could give the Silent Treatment, too. Without a word, I picked my way past them all, and headed back to my kennel.

CHAPTER 4

THE NEXT FEW DAYS were the loneliest of my life. To be with the animals you've worked and lived with since you were a puppy, and not one of them will so much as look at you? Man, it bites.

The ringmaster had pulled the "Pete and Rita" act after that disastrous show. I was back working with the Performing Pups. At least, I was trying to. It's hard, when you're invisible.

The problems started at rehearsal. On cue, Bob, Lolly, and I came hopping out on our hind legs.

Mike tossed Bob a big red rubber ring. Mike raised his arm. Bob tossed the ring to Lolly, who caught it. Mike raised his arm again. That was the signal for Lolly to toss it to me. But instead, she threw it back to Bob!

Mike tootled a little silver whistle, "*Tweet!*" which means "no." Taking the ring from Bob, Mike tossed it to me. I caught it. Now what?

Mike raised his arm. I looked at Bob and Lolly. Neither of them was looking at me.

I could tell Mike was getting peeved. He raised his arm again and snapped, "Pete! Toss!" Like it was my fault! I couldn't disobey a direct command. Besides, I was starting to drool. I tossed the ring to Bob. Who let it fall—flop!—at his feet.

"Just do the trick, okay?" I snarled. "You're making us look like idiots!"

Bob asked, "Did you hear something?"

Lolly scratched her ear. "Not a thing," she said.

If dogs could grind their teeth, mine would have been a pile of powder.

"Hey, guys? I hope you're enjoying this, because the audience sure won't." I flopped down on the sawdust, seething. Mike squatted down.

"What's the matter with you, Pete? You sick or somethin'?"

"Yeah. Sick of these amateurs," I snorted. Mike couldn't understand me, but I saw Bob's ears twitch.

Good. Mike snapped his fingers and pointed to the exit. I scooted out.

Let Lolly and Bob do the heavy lifting. Between my last performance and the Silent Treatment, I'd had enough.

But I'd forgotten one of the oldest circus superstitions. Bad luck always comes in threes.

"Greta?" Mike called to his wife, who was teaching Arthur to push a wheelbarrow. She looked up. "Take Pete and give him his dinner, if he'll eat it. Something's up with him, but I'll be darned if I know what."

Greta led me to their trailer. "You can camp with us, honey, till we see what the trouble is," she said. "Just a little food, though, in case it don't sit good."

She filled a bowl half full of kibbles, and I tucked in. Who needs other dogs? Not me. There was a nice little throw rug calling my name. I curled up on it and went to sleep.

That evening, Mike checked me out good. He looked in my ears, down my throat, then ran his hands over me. There was nothing to find. Mike has a way of plucking at his hair when he's worried. Right now it was standing on end like a bristle brush.

"You don't think he's gettin' addled, do you?"

Addled? What did that mean?

"Like, nuts or something?" Greta asked. To my horror, Mike nodded.

"Sometimes a purebred dog can nut up on you. Remember Rocky?"

Yikes! I remembered Rocky. He was a big old wirehaired terrier. One day he woke up from a nap, yelping that invisible rats were biting him. He started snapping at the air. Then he chased his tail until he fell over. That performance got him a one-way ticket out of show business. He hasn't been heard from since.

Between Marvo and Rocky, my future with the circus wasn't looking so bright. I edged over to Mike and licked his hand. Mike petted me, then went back to tweaking his hair.

After dinner, Mike and Greta let me curl up on the sofa with them and watch TV. I was half asleep, enjoying one of Greta's great back scratches, when she suddenly stopped.

"Why do they call her the Airhead Heiress?" Greta asked.

"Because she's got millions of dollars and no sense," Mike explained. They both giggled at that.

I nosed Greta's hand so she'd get back to my back

scratch. But my ears pricked up at the word "dognappers . . ."

". . . who earlier today snatched Lacie Whyte's pet
Chihuahua, Baby," the news guy was saying. Behind
him was a picture of the heiress, clutching what looked
like a shaved rat in a pink angora sweater. The pop-
eyed pup even sported a swanky diamond collar. Bling!

"Baby was grabbed when Ms. Whyte's personal
maid, Quinn Carey, had it out for a walk," he contin-
ued. "So far, police are clueless."

The camera cut to Lacie Whyte, standing in front of a bunch of cameras. She was tall and skinny, with long yellow hair she kept flipping back. "If the dognappers are, like, watching? Please, please, bring Baby back. Because I am, like, so totally bummed right now!" And she broke down sobbing. A couple of beefy guys in sunglasses led her to her limo.

I'm a sentimental hound, and this touched my heart. Poor Baby. Pinched from her pink silken pillow, lifted from the lap of luxury. Probably ate bonbons all day out of a pink bowl. Bet nobody gave her the Silent Treatment. Or barked orders at her.

Curled up in my bed that night, I thought about it. Maybe being a pet wasn't so bad, if you could get yourself a human like the Airhead Heiress. Who was certainly in need of a new dog.

A talented one, who could do awesome tricks. And was already tinted her favorite color!

It suddenly hit me how nutty the whole notion was. Me, a pet? Get a grip! I was circus, all the way to the bone. I just had to get out of the doghouse and back on top of the bill.

CHAPTER **5**

AFTER THE PUPS rejected me, I figured the ring-master would kick me down to the clown act again. The last time I'd worked with them it had been as the Canine Cannonball. Getting shot from a cannon two shows a day was the lowest I'd ever sunk in show-biz. If I never wore that crash helmet again, it would be too soon. So I was relieved when Mike decided I should do a bit with the Lipizzaner sisters. He told their trainer, Madame Suzette, "For some reason he just ain't working with the other dogs."

Madame frowned, tapping her chin. "Eez possible. He eez fast learner, no?"

"Sure! Pete's so smart, he's almost human sometimes."

I knew he meant that as a compliment, so I took no offense.

I also knew that the chances of the Lipizzaner mares working with me were about as good as a snow cone's in August.

Madame led Czarina out. The mare had a special saddle on, like a little platform. Madame set a short ladder against Czarina's side and whistled at me. I scrambled up, but not fast enough. Czarina took a giant step to the left, and suddenly I was scrambling in air. *Boom!* I landed spread-eagled on the floor.

Madame clucked impatiently. She took a firm grip on Czarina's bridle and whistled. Again, I went up the ladder. Czarina quivered, but stood her ground. Very carefully, I sat.

"I hope you don't think this was my idea," I hissed.

Czarina, of course, ignored me.

Madame snapped her riding crop twice against her boot, and Czarina broke into a canter, then a gallop. I could hear Madame shouting at her to slow down.

'Round the ring we pounded, me hunkered down in mortal terror. Czarina was picking up speed with every step. The air whistled through my fur. The bleachers whizzed by in a blur. Something told me this couldn't last.

It didn't.

As suddenly as she'd giddyupped, Czarina whoa'd. I went flying top over tail and hit the sawdust so hard I saw stars. Where was that darn helmet when I needed it? When I finally stopped rolling, I dragged myself to my feet.

"Call yourself a thoroughbred?" I scoffed. "I've seen cement trucks with a smoother ride!" I braced myself, expecting a kick.

But that nag never stirred, not so much as an ear. Madame hustled over to her, scolding in shrill Polish. Czarina let herself be led off, gentle as a lamb, and didn't even look back.

I shook my head to get the last of the sawdust out of my ears.

This Silent Treatment stuff was getting old.

A little voice whispered in my head. It said maybe it was time to swallow my pride, apologize to Rita, and get back to business. Then I remembered how she'd made me look like a dope, for cheap laughs. Where was her apology to me? The little voice shut up.

Poor Madame Suzette! She had to explain to Mike and the ringmaster why her brilliant horse had shot me off her back like a cannonball. Of course, she couldn't.

"Is mystery! Czarina is good girl alvhays, no problem making. But zhis poodle, she vill not carry. I cannot tell vhy not!"

The ringmaster rubbed his sweaty head with his bandanna and made a sour face. "Somethin' ain't right with that dog."

The three of them peered at me. I offered a paw to shake. Nobody took it.

Just then, a powerful gust of wind made the tent canvas shiver.

"Guy on the radio said a big blow's gonna pass through here," the ringmaster said.

Madame shivered, too. "Sounds like it vants to take tent vhiz it."

"Start packing up," the ringmaster ordered. "We're pulling out as soon as the canvas crew can tear down." He gave me a fishy look. "Keep that dog in line, Mike, or else. I've had all the surprises outta him I'm gonna take."

Mike nodded, snapped his fingers, and I followed him out of the tent to his camper. Behind us the roustabouts were already hauling down the short poles, in a hurry to get the big top put away.

Greta stowed the lawn chairs in the camper, then Mike helped her roll up the awning.

"You travel with us, boy," Mike said, pausing to ruffle my ears. That was good news. Let the rest of the dogs ride in the smelly old circus train. I'd be traveling in style with my real friends. My only friends. Who needed animals, anyhow? I had humans! Humans who loved me, and petted me, and shared their chow. Humans who . . .

"I'm thinking we're gonna have to leave Pete behind next year, Greta."

My heart skipped a beat. Leave? Pete? Behind?

"Yeah, it's looking that way," she said.

Huh?! *Et tu,* Greta?

A fat raindrop splashed on my nose. I looked up. The sky was a muddy green, like a dirty copper bowl. A swirl of dust churned up around us. Suddenly, it felt much colder. Had winter decided to make a surprise appearance?

Mike was already holding the camper's back door open for me. I clambered in. Greta started the engine as Mike hopped into the passenger seat. We pulled out of the field and onto the paved road. Mike slid open the little window between the cab and the camper.

"You okay, Pete?"

I turned my back on him. I could give the Silent Treatment, too.

"Mike, you think it's safe to drive?" Greta worried.

"There's the ringmaster's camper up ahead. We'll follow him. If it does hit, the middle of an open field ain't exactly where you want to be," Mike pointed out.

Putting my paws up on the sofa back, I watched out of the window as we drove onto the freeway. Gee, it was dark. It looked like midnight, and I hadn't even had lunch yet.

I could see the ringmaster's taillights up ahead of us. I heard a distant rumble. A raindrop plopped on the windshield, then another. Greta switched on the wipers. All at once, it was pouring.

Mike snapped on the radio. There was a crackle and hiss, then a wavering siren. Then another angry crackle. Then nothing but hiss. Mike turned it off.

"I got a bad feeling about this," Mike muttered. I could feel the camper move sideways on the road, like something was shoving it.

Greta's hands were clamped on the wheel so hard her knuckles shone white.

Rain thrummed the roof like a drumroll. As dark as it had been, it was getting darker.

Up ahead, I could just make out a cement overpass. The ringmaster's camper pulled over underneath it. Greta parked behind him. Mike jumped out of the cab. He and the ringmaster talked a moment, then Mike came sprinting back.

"Twister's coming! We gotta stay here!"

Greta moaned. "Out here in the open?"

"It's too close. We're better off under this bridge than on the road."

What was a twister, anyway? It sounded like a carnival ride. Or something to eat. And speaking of eats, when was I gonna get my lunch? It wasn't enough they were going to abandon me. Did they have to starve me, too?

Irritated, I let out a sharp bark. They must have forgotten I was even there because they both jumped.

Mike turned around, furious. "Quiet!"

Surprised, I let out a growl. A little one. It was enough for Mike. Smack! Right on the muzzle. Then he shut the window between us with a bang.

Nice. Real nice.

Bad dog, Pete. Quiet, Pete. Disappear, why don't you, Pete?

Well, why didn't I?

That's when it hit me! I knew how to put Mike and all my furry fair-weather friends in their places. How to make them sorry that they'd turned on me.

I'd run away!

CHAPTER 6

THE SECOND THE IDEA came to me, I knew I'd do it. I'd pull a disappearing act. And without a word to anyone. They wouldn't have Pierre Le Chien to nose-smack anymore. By the time they realized I was gone, I'd be far from their stupid old circus. Not to mention that upstaging ape, Rita. Oh, yeah, they'd all be sorry then.

But it would be too late.

I could just picture it. All the dogs with their heads in their paws, howling. "Dear old Pete! How could we have been such fools?"

I'd show those snooty Lipizzaner sisters, who'd been so quick to take Rita's side against *moi*. I'd give that motormouthed feather duster, PeeWee, something to blab about. Would Zamba lose his appetite, thinking of his old pal adrift in the storm? Would Lucky's guilty conscience keep him awake? Or, at least, give him nightmares?

Just thinking about it made me feel better. I decided to go now, before I changed my mind.

Mike was hunkered down with Greta in the cab. The back door of the camper was probably unlocked. All I had to do was paw at the knob until . . .

The door blew open with a bang. I glanced back at Mike and Greta. Had they heard it? Nope. I stuck my head out and a gust flattened my fur. The rain was blowing sideways in big wavy sheets. Whatever a twister was, it sure made a fuss getting here. Hey!— were those cornstalks actually *hopping* across the freeway? I'd seen stormy weather in my time, but this was a real showstopper. Well, it wasn't gonna stop my show.

I jumped out of the camper. The wind was even worse than I'd thought. I had to crouch down to keep from being blown onto the freeway. Not that there were any cars in sight. Where had everybody gone? There were those freaky cornstalks, with hay bales rolling after them like stampeding buffalos.

Like they were all running from something.

At that very moment, something jerked my tail. I whirled, expecting to see the twister behind me.

Worse. It was Rita.

"What are you doing out here?" she demanded.

"If I was speaking to you, which I ain't, I could ask you the same thing!"

"I caught a ride with the ringmaster. I saw you out the window. Why aren't you in the camper?"

"I'm blowing this pop stand. Checking out. Exit, laughing." I grinned, or tried to. A twig blew into my mouth. I spat it out.

"You're kidding!"

"Nope."

"Then you're nuts. Nobody runs away *from* the circus!"

"Watch me," I snapped. I kept walking. Rita, stubborn as ever, stuck to me like a burr.

"You're bluffing."

"I'm gonna find a nice new owner. Somebody who'll give me steak bones and lots of belly rubs. Somebody loyal. Unlike some I could mention."

Rita stared. "You—*you*—are going to be a *pet*?!"

Hearing her say it out loud, it hit me what a totally

stupid idea it really was. But I couldn't back down now! Rita would never let me hear the end of it.

"You're smarter than you look, Banana Breath."

"Oh, please!" she scoffed. "You? Rolling over, begging for a biscuit? Don't make me laugh!"

"Beats mud wrestling with crazy apes."

"People want puppies."

"I'm house trained. I don't chew slippers. I don't have fleas. And I do tricks. Good ones. Some lucky family's gonna grab me faster than you can say, 'So long, suckers.'"

By this time we were both yelling—not because we were mad, but because the wind was blowing so bad we could hardly hear each other.

Suddenly Rita screamed and lunged into me, tumbling us both off the road and into a ditch. Just in time, too. A full-grown tree, limbs thrashing, went roaring by right where we'd been standing!

I'd never seen a flying tree. I hope I never see another one. If Rita hadn't pulled me out of its path, I'd have been a poodle puddle.

I was about to thank her, when the freight train hit us.

CHAPTER 7

AT LEAST, IT SOUNDED like a freight train. It was the biggest booming roar you can imagine, so deep it hurt my ears.

Whining, I looked up at Rita, who still had her arms clenched around my neck. "Okay, you win!" I yelped. "Let's go back!"

Rita was staring past me, eyes popping with fear. "Hold on!" she squawked.

I looked in the direction she was looking. A huge black funnel daggered down from the sky, dragging the ground, coming straight at us.

An instant later, I was sucked up into the clouds.

Darkness dropped over me like a blanket. I couldn't breathe. My legs pumped wildly, but there was no earth under my paws. Stuff was swirling through the air around me—pieces of board, a tire off a car. Dirt, dust, and water beat at my face and belly. Wind slapped me like a cat slaps a yarn ball. I squeezed my eyes tight. Rita was practically strangling me. All I could hear was the roar and her scream.

Then, I passed out.

When I came to, every bone in my body was barking. It took a real effort to lift my lids and survey the damage.

The first clue that I wasn't where I was supposed to be was the crow staring back at me, eyeball to eyeball. He looked as surprised as I was. Maybe more. A quick glance around told me why.

I was up a tree.

I've been a of lot places, but up a tree was something new. My hindquarters were wedged into a forked limb, and my front end was being held up by a tangle of branches. Trying to move as little as possible, I peered down through the leaves.

Oooh. This was a *big* tree.

There was a meadow under me. But "down" looked a long way off. The grass was shiny wet, and muddy puddles were scattered here and there. Beyond the meadow, I saw . . . corn. Fields of it, miles of it, stretching out in all directions. Just . . . corn.

The crow gave a rattling caw and flew off. I wished I could do the same.

"Not from around here, are you?"

With an effort, I craned my neck to see who was talking. A pair of black horses, as alike as two eggs in a nest, stared up at me.

"Bingo. How can you tell?"

"Don't see dogs in trees in these parts. Can't climb 'em."

"Cats climb 'em, Prince," offered the second horse.

"Yup. But not dogs, Coaly," the first one agreed.

"Nope. Nor sheep, nor cows, neither," the second horse concurred.

"Nope. Nor pigs . . ."

I could see they were ready to run through the whole list of non-tree-climbing animals, so I cut in.

"You guys think we could talk about this later? Like, after you get me down?"

"'Nother thing, Coaly," the first horse went on, like he hadn't heard me. "Dogs around here ain't pink."

"Nope. Nor horses. Nor cows . . ."

"Nope. Nor sheep . . ."

"Hello? Up here? In the tree? Little help?!"

The horses swung their long heads back and forth.

"Can't help ye," the first one, Coaly, said. "No getting a horse into a tree."

"There's a good-sized puddle down t'other side," Prince offered. "Maybe you can jump down and aim for that."

A puddle? My heart leaped. In my early years as the star of Moliere's Performing Pups, my act had been jumping through a flaming hoop and into a kiddie pool. A puddle couldn't be much smaller than a kiddie pool.

Could it?

Carefully, with twigs snapping noisily all around, I edged my way across the canopy of limbs holding me up. A paw slipped through. I froze. But there was no place to go except forward. Inch by inch, I crept. Not many dogs could have done it. But I, Pierre Le Chien, am not many dogs.

Gritting my teeth, I looked down again.

There was the puddle.

One deep breath to steady myself and—I leaped!

For the second time that day, I was flying. I didn't

like it any better this time. *Splash!* I hit the puddle.

It was deeper than it looked, a regular mud hole. I clambered up its slick side, panting and coated with slime.

As I lay there, collecting my wits, the two horses ambled over.

Coaly said, "Well, you ain't pink no more. How'd you get up there, anyhow?"

"I flew."

"You one of them aliens?" Prince asked.

"You could say that. Any chance of some dinner?"

The horses looked at each other, then at me. "Maybe."

I shook myself, scattering muddy droplets. "Great. Take me to your feeder."

Coaly turned back to Prince. "Reckon we oughta take him to Miz Shaw?"

Prince snorted thoughtfully. "We best take him to Buck. Buck'll know what to do." Without another word, they turned together and started walking across the field. I trotted along behind them.

No matter what Buck was, he couldn't be any worse than a twister. But where was I? Even more worrying, where was everyone else?

CHAPTER 8

I **FIGURED THIS BUCK** they were taking me to was their owner. But he was a barrel-chested mutt with a flat face, mean little eyes, and a coat like an old carpet. He circled me slowly, sniffing at me longer than good manners allow.

"You're one funny-lookin' dog," he said finally. "You better get away before ol' Miz Shaw takes a shot at you. She don't like stray dogs. Says they're chicken thieves. You a chicken thief, boy?"

"No!"

Out of the corner of my eye, I saw something white edging up on me. I turned to look. A big lopsided duck stood eyeing me from a safe distance.

"What about ducks?" it quacked nervously. "Ask him if he's a duck thief."

"I'm no kind of thief, buddy. I work for my living."

Buck smiled. His teeth needed brushing. But there were plenty of them. "Me, too. My work's keeping varmints off the place."

"What's a varmint?"

"Any animal that don't belong and ain't wanted. Like you."

I heard the screen door of the farmhouse open and whirled to see a little old human lady come out. She was carrying a bucket. This must be Miz Shaw! She stopped, surprised. I wagged my tail, eager to show her I was not the chicken-snatching type.

Buck picked that moment to jump me. Suddenly we were rolling around in the dirt, him trying to get his fangs into my throat. Miz Shaw was yelling at Buck to stop, but he wasn't listening.

A bucket of cold water hit us. That got through to Buck, who let me up. He made a big show of standing there, snarling, with his neck hair all fluffed out.

"Tough guy, huh?" I snarled. "Next time, let me know you're coming and I'll have something ready for ya!"

Miz Shaw came slowly toward me, her hand out. I'd expected a gun-toting battle-ax. Not this trim little granny in a pink track suit. Her hair was a pleasing shade of lavender and curly like mine. She smelled nice, too. Like pie. Cherry.

"Who we got here?" she clucked. She patted my head, and I licked her hand. Yep, cherry.

"You lost, puppy?" She felt my neck for a collar, but I wasn't wearing one. "You been rollin' in the mud, I reckon. Come on."

She headed toward the barn, and I happily followed her. Buck slunk behind us. The duck loped along behind Buck. Inside the barn, Miz Shaw grabbed a dusty wash pan off a workbench. She filled it with dog food from a covered barrel and set it on the floor. I didn't wait to be asked twice. She watched as I polished off the food, then gave me another pat on the head.

"You're a cute lil' old fella, ain't cha? What's your name?"

"Pete!" I barked. Of course, she couldn't understand me, but she laughed.

"Smart, too, I reckon. Shake hands?"

I stuck out a paw. She laughed again. "Now look at that!"

She liked tricks? I'd give her tricks. I spotted an empty barrel on its side. Showtime!

I trotted over to it and jumped up. Barrel rolling is puppy stuff for a pro like me. I rolled that barrel toward her, then back, paddling my paws as fast as I could. She gasped, clasping her hands in awe. I sprang off the barrel, did a midair somersault and kangaroo

hopped over to her on my hind legs. Then I sat down to catch my breath.

"My land!" Miz Shaw turned to Buck. "You see that, Buck? This here dog is somethin' special. Don't you fight him no more."

She bent down to give me a good pat. "I never did see a dog do such fancy tricks. I think I'll call you Trixie."

I could hear Buck snort behind me.

"Somebody'll be lookin' for you, sure as you're born. Until they find you, you just stay with us." She took Buck by the collar and pulled him over to me. "Now you two make friends," she said. Buck sighed, but didn't try to bite me.

"Truce?" I offered.

Buck snorted again. "Whatever you say, Trixie."

Miz Shaw let him loose, satisfied. "Good boy, Buck. Trixie will be nice company for you."

Buck shot me a dirty look. "I reckon I got to put up with you. But you best leave them chickens be." He sauntered off.

"Hey, Trixie?" It was that lopsided duck again.

"Pete. Call me Pete."

"Where'd you learn to do that fancy stuff?"

"Under the big top, my fowl friend. Circus Martinez."

The duck blinked his beady eyes. His beak gaped.

"You—you're in show business. For real?"

"I was, until I blew into this burg. Which is where, by the way?"

"This here's Walnut Hill. I know all about show business."

"Yeah? How so?"

The duck puffed his chest out proudly. "I watch TV! Set right up on that there window ledge, purt' near every night." He jutted his head toward me. "I'm working on an act myself. Gonna try out for one of them amateur programs. Maybe you'd like to see."

Not. "Another time."

He looked deflated. "Okay. But, Trixie? I'd watch out for Buck. I don't think he likes you."

That hick? I smirked. "I ain't planning to stay long. He doesn't have to like me. He just has to live with me."

But Buck had no intention of doing either.

CHAPTER 9

I **SPENT THAT NIGHT** on a folded blanket in a corner of Miz Shaw's back porch. Tired as I was by the day's adventures, I had a hard time getting to sleep.

They say the country is quiet. They're wrong. There are all kinds of noises, mostly creepy. I thought of the circus train and my cozy basket. The jumbled perfumes of lion, horse, dog, and warm hay. The rustles and snores of sleeping animals. Wrapped in happy memories, I slept.

I am not by nature an early riser. Buck was. At dawn he nipped my ear.

"Rise and shine, Trixie!"

I rose, all right, straight into the air. Buck about choked laughing.

"You got work to do, boy. You want Miz Shaw to think you're worth feeding, don't you?"

I stretched and yawned. "What kind of work?"

Buck eyed me thoughtfully. "Well, I don't expect you're much of a rat killer, are you?"

"Certainly not." The idea made my blood run cold.

"Maybe you could learn to weed."

If this bozo could do it, I could, too, and better.

"Lead on, Professor." I sniffed. Buck trotted off. I followed him to a dirt patch in front of the house, where a few plants were scattered.

"This here's Miz Shaw's flower bed. But it's all full of weeds. See?" He scratched at one of the plants, and then jerked it out of the ground. "Reckon you can do that?"

Was he kidding? I shouldered him aside. I grabbed one of the plants and tossed it halfway across the yard. "Like that?"

"You sure catch on fast." Buck shook his head admiringly.

I was pulling out another one when someone nipped my tail. *Youch!* I whirled to confront the sneak attacker.

It was that wacky duck again! He was so excited, he was hopping from one foot to the other.

"Them's Miz Shaw's zinnias!"

"Shut your yap, Quackers!" Buck snarled.

"She ain't gonna like you pullin' them up, Trixie," Quackers squeaked. "She's liable to—"

There was a noise inside the house. Buck's head jerked up. Then he was gone like a shot.

The screen door banged open. Miz Shaw stuck her head out. She saw me standing there with a zinnia in my mouth.

And screamed bloody murder.

"My zinnias! Why, you . . ." That sweet little old lady snatched up a hoe and came after me. She was nimble, but I had her beat for speed. By the time she was worn out chasing me, she'd gotten over being mad. She flopped down on a lawn chair, fanning herself with her hand. I edged over to her and laid my head on her knee. I didn't have to fake feeling sorry. I *was* sorry.

"Well, I reckon you don't know no better. But you do that again, and I'll skin you. Hear?"

I heard.

Quackers waddled up. "I tried to tell you, buddy. You gotta watch out for Buck. Hey, did you want me to show you my—"

"Thanks, duck. I owe you one. I owe Buck one, too." Bristling, I stalked off to go Buck hunting.

I found him sprawled in the shade of an old tractor, behind the barn.

"What's the big idea? Trying to make me look bad in front of the boss?" I demanded.

Buck grinned. "Is it my fault you don't know a weed from a flower, Trixie? And you so smart and all."

I started to walk away, but he stopped me.

"Aw, don't get your tail in a twist. I was just kiddin'. Teach me that barrel trick, would ya?"

"How 'bout I teach you to disappear?"

"Hey, I said I was sorry, didn't I? Look, I'll take you out with me tonight, show you how to run off varmints. Miz Shaw sure would appreciate that. She'll forget all about them zinnias."

That sounded fair. Maybe I just didn't get country humor or something. Buck's tail was wagging. I gave a wag back. A little one.

"Okay."

The afternoon dragged by. The heat didn't help. I went looking for somewhere to cool off and sniffed out a pond. Coaly and Prince were already there, up to their knees in the muddy water.

"Looky 'ere, Prince. It's that flyin' dog," Coaly said.

Prince nodded to me. "Water's nice. Come on in."

I hopped in for a quick dip and managed to get some of the mud off me. But my nice pink fur was still stained a nasty brown. It would take Greta hours to get it clean . . .

The thought of Greta stabbed at my heart like a knife. All the years she and Mike had cared for me came back in a rush. Why had I wanted to leave them? The faces of my friends seemed to float up before me. Imelda, Sophie, Czarina. Good old Lucky and Zamba. Gosh, I missed the Pups, every one of them! If only I could hear PeeWee honking at me again. But would I?

And Rita. What about Rita? My conscience gnawed me like a bone. I'd bitten Rita, and how had she paid me back? By risking her own neck to save mine when the storm hit.

Where was she now?

I was lucky to be alive. Maybe she hadn't been so lucky.

Maybe nobody had.

I pulled myself onto the bank and rolled in the grass. How could I have wanted for one second to be a pet? Rita was right. My home was that big striped circus tent.

This was no place like home.

I moaned, closing my eyes. Misery washed over me like muddy water.

"Howdy, Trixie! I've been lookin' for you," someone quacked. I opened my eyes to see the duck barreling toward me. "Been workin' on my impressions. Guess what this one is?" Ruffling his feathers up, he squeezed his eyes closed. "Mwack! Mmwack! Mmmwa-a-ack."

"Uh—a duck chewing gum?"

His wings drooped. "Naw! A cow. Ain't you never heard a cow? How 'bout this one? Bw-ack! bw-ack!" He stopped, looking pleased. "That's a dog. For my act, remember?"

I remembered. "Look—uh—what's your name?"

He marched over to me, cheerful again. "Miz Shaw calls me Quackers. But I'll prob'ly change it when I break into showbiz."

Oy, what was it with this quackpot and showbiz? "Listen, Quackers. You said this place was called Walnut Hill. Where is that exactly?"

"Kansas. Don't you know nothin'?"

My heart fell. "Whoa. That's a long way from Florida."

"What's Florida?"

"Where my circus goes for the off-season. I've got to get back to them."

Quackers cocked his little head to the side. "Reckon I could go with you? Try out my act when we get there?"

I didn't want to rain on his parade, but a duck in the circus? Much less one that does bad impressions? I didn't think so.

"I don't even know how I'm gonna get there, pal." That was true. We'd played Kansas. I knew that Florida was south—but which way was south? I figured it would have been four or five days' ride on the train, not counting stops.

How long would it take on four feet?

CHAPTER **10**

THERE HAD TO BE a way to get home. Surely a lucky break would come my way. A truck, a train, a talent scout—who knew? I needed to keep up my strength, greet Opportunity when it knocked.

Miz Shaw could be grouchy, but she was great when it came to the grub. Whatever she didn't eat, she gave to Buck and me. That evening it was leftover biscuits and gravy. When she came out with the fry pan, Buck's mouth watered so hard he practically slipped in it. He fell on his food like he was starving. Then he watched me eat, little eyes narrowed. I ate slowly, savoring every yummy mouthful. After delicately licking the bowl, I sighed and flopped down, satisfied.

"If it wasn't for you, all that woulda been mine,"

Buck growled. "You gonna start earning your keep tonight. I'm takin' you varmint hunting."

"Sure," I agreed. Man, this country mutt had a one-track mind.

"Let's go." Buck ambled off into the darkness. I got up and followed him.

It was a beautiful night. The moon was bright as a silver platter. We worked our way around the back of the property. I sniffed, catching the scent of ripe tomatoes.

"That's Miz Shaw's vegetable patch," Buck hissed. "Something's in there. Get down!"

We dropped to our bellies.

I caught sight of it first. Black and white. A small head, short legs, a fluffy tail.

"What is that thing? Some kind of cat?" I whispered.

Buck gave me a sidelong look. "Uh . . . yep. Polecat. Reckon you can take him?"

"You kidding?" What self-respecting dog couldn't roust a cat?

"Ah, you're all bark, Trixie." I could see his gleaming grin.

"Oh, yeah? Watch. And quit calling me Trixie!"

I crept forward. The polecat was rooting around a

lettuce plant. He didn't hear me coming.

I sprang out to face him, barking like crazy. I'd show Buck how much dog I was!

But this crazy cat just stood there, staring at me.

I stopped barking. "What are you, nuts?" I snarled. I could hear Buck snickering. Laugh, would he? I'd show them both!

I lunged at the cat.

Who, instead of taking off, turned around and lifted his fluffy tail. I was a hair's length from chomping on it, when he let fly with . . .

Well, I don't what. A secret weapon? Poison gas? The world's stinkiest stink bomb? Whatever it was, it worked. I lost all interest in varmint hunting.

My eyes were aflame! My nose felt like a firecracker had gone off in it. My fur seemed to writhe. Buck was rolling around, laughing his dumb head off. I staggered over to him.

"What . . . what kind of a cat did you say that was?!" I gasped.

"Polecat! Pooo-ee!" He ran off.

Tail between my legs, I went scratching at Miz Shaw's door for help. She opened it long enough to slam it in my face.

"Git!" she screeched. "You been skunked!"

I couldn't blame her. I could hardly stand myself.

I galloped to the pond and plunged in. A few laps later, I got out and shook myself. The bath hadn't helped. If anything, I smelled worse. What I needed was a place to hide until it wore off.

Out back of the barn, I saw an old wooden lean-to. Inside, I found what looked like a big hole in the ground, with rough stairs leading into it.

Carefully I picked my way down them into the darkness. I stood at the bottom in a shaft of moonlight and looked around. A bag of onions hung from a rafter. Dusty jars of preserves lined wooden shelves. This seemed like a good place to be alone.

But something told me I wasn't alone.

A rustle, a breath . . . I couldn't smell them over the skunk stink, but I was sure they could smell me.

"Who's there?" I growled, trying to sound tough. I listened.

Silence.

Then, without warning, a jar of peaches went flying by my head, smashing against the dirt wall behind me! I yelped and ducked. A jar of tomatoes came hurtling out of the darkness, exploding like a grenade at my feet. Whoever was down here could have been pitching for the majors.

"Whaddaya trying to do, pal? Win a teddy bear?!" I snarled.

As suddenly as it had started, the bombardment stopped. I could hear something coming slowly toward me. It spoke.

"P-pete?!"

MY EARS POPPED UP. My jaw hit the ground.
I knew that voice as well as my own.

"Rita?!"

There she was, bounding at me. Before I could react, she tackled me, hugging and chittering hysterically. I was so happy to see her, I licked her ugly face.

"You're alive!" we said at the same time.

"I fell into a tree—"

"I thought you were dead!"

"Me, too!"

Rita let go and took a giant step back, rubbing her nose. "Dawg, what have you been rolling in? You stink like last week's roadkill."

"They got cats here, that . . . Never mind, you wouldn't believe me."

We went up the steps into the moonlight, talking excitedly. Rita was at the part where the twister had dumped her into a mound of warm cow plop.

"It wouldn't have been my first choice. But it beat hitting the cow." She'd found the cellar and had been living on Miz Shaw's preserves. "The spiced peaches are particularly fine."

Just then, a voice piped up out of the darkness, making both of us nearly jump out of our skins. "Trixie! What *is* that thing?!"

I whirled to see Quackers staring goggle-eyed at Rita.

"Trixie? Who's Trixie?" Rita asked.

"Who're you?" Quackers demanded.

"This is Rita, from the circus. She's a chimp."

"From the circus?" Quackers fluffed up and toddled over to have a better look. When he got close, Rita reached over and flicked his beak. Quackers retreated, looking miffed.

"Take a picture, it'll last longer," Rita snapped.

"Rita's my partner." It felt good to say that again.

"Pete, where are we?" Rita turned to me.

"Walnut Hill, Kansas!" Quackers piped up.

"Florida's south, I know that much," I said.

"Then south we go. Uh—which way is south?" Rita added.

I shook my head. "We'll just have to figure it out as we go, I guess." It didn't sound so far-fetched, now that Rita was with me. "Take care of yourself, duck. Give my regards to Buck."

"Wait!" Quackers quacked. "Take me with you!"

Rita raised her eyebrows. "Why would we do that?"

"I want to be in the circus, too! Tell her 'bout my act!"

"He—he does impressions."

"Listen!" Quackers screwed up his eyes and cocked his head back. "Mwaa-ack! Mwaa-ack!" He stopped, looking pleased. "What did that sound like?"

"I'd hate to tell you."

Quackers blinked in surprise. "Trixie couldn't tell it, either. Don't you have cows where you come from? But that ain't all! I can dance. Looky here."

Quackers started flapping those big flat feet, stretching out his wings. Hopping and flopping, he whirled and leaped like he was dodging a phantom weasel. Finally he quit, gasping for breath. There were so many feathers flying, it looked like a pillow fight. Rita stared at him with something like awe.

"Quackers, old fowl, you've got it."

Quackers brightened. "I do?!"

Rita nodded. "Yep. And you can keep it. Come on, Pete."

We started off, but Quackers wasn't giving up. "You'll never get there. You don't know the way!" he squawked. "I do!"

That stopped us.

"What do you mean, you do?" I asked.

"I'm a duck, see? Ducks fly south for the winter. South!"

Rita waved him off. "Wild ducks. You're a tame duck."

"Yeah, but all ducks know where south is. It's whatchamacallit—instinct." He puffed out his feathers, preening. "You need me."

Rita and I looked at each other. "Hmm. He's got a point. Unless dogs have a built-in compass, too?" Rita said.

I shook my head. "Looks like we're taking the duck."

Quackers made a happy honk-honk-honking noise. Rita covered her ears, and he stopped.

"Couple of things," she snapped, poking him in the chest. "First of all, you do what we say. No arguments. You're in charge of directions, and that's it. Second, a word to the wise? Keep your day job. You're not show-biz material."

Quackers looked downcast, but only for a moment. "Well, I got the whole trip to change your mind."

Rita groaned. "That's what I'm afraid of."

CHAPTER 12

R ITA SAID WE COULD only travel at night, since the natives wouldn't take kindly to a chimp running loose. But Quackers slowed us down considerably. Ducks aren't too fleet of foot, and Quackers was slower than most.

"Bein' as how I got one short leg," he explained.

Rita sniffed. "What are the wings for? Decoration?"

"I can fly!" Quackers said. "Jus' not too far." He started flapping his wings. It took all he had to make liftoff. A few yards along, he hit the ground with a thud. He couldn't keep that up for long, and pretty soon he was limping along behind again.

Finally he stopped. "I can't walk no more. My feet ain't made for it."

Rita glared at him. "You're kind of an odd duck. Wings you can't fly with and feet you can't walk on. What do you want us to do? Carry you?"

Quackers brightened up. "Could ya?"

Rita glared at him, then at me. But she picked Quackers up and held him tight under one arm. Quackers wriggled. Rita clamped him harder.

"You're chokin' me!" he squawked.

"If only," Rita sighed. But she loosed her grip.

We kept going until dawn's rosy fingers waved in the east. A mowed field dotted with haystacks glowed pink in the morning light. We found ourselves a cozy pile of hay away from the road and dug in to its sweet-smelling warmth. There's no nicer bed than clean hay, no matter what kind of animal you are. The last thing I heard was the sound of my own snoring.

It must have been hours later when I lifted my head again. I shook off the clinging hay and looked around. There was Quackers, already up and pecking his break-fast out of the stubble. He saw me and waved a wing.

"Trix—I mean, Pete, there's plenty good bugs, if you're hungry."

I sneezed out a snoot full of hay dust. "They're all yours, duck. Dogs crave bigger game."

Rita sat up beside me, cleaning an ear with one lazy finger. She blinked at the afternoon sky and sniffed.

"Your perfume must be wearing off. I smell apples."

It didn't take us long to sniff out the orchard. The day was heating up, but the grass was cool and lush under the trees. Quackers stuffed himself on snails as Rita and I picked through the windfalls. I sprawled in the grass, belly full of apples. Rita hauled herself to the top of a tree and peered around.

"Hey, duck. Which direction is south?" she called down.

Quackers paused and cocked his head like he could hear something we couldn't. Then he nodded and pointed with his wing. "Attaway."

Rita hopped down from the tree. "Well, then, looks like we caught ourselves a break, boys. Just happens there's a river over there. And I think it's going our way."

She was right! All of a sudden, I could smell it on the breeze. The chocolaty tang of mud, rotten wood, and water weeds. A greenish-brown aroma, as rich as cake. As we came over a hill, there it was. Murky, alive, moving—and so big across that the few boats on it looked like bathtub toys. Rita and I stood and gaped, then gaped some more.

Quackers trotted to the edge and hopped right in. "Come on, you guys!"

Rita and I clambered to the bank. Rita stuck a toe in, and pulled it out fast. "I just remembered. Chimps don't swim." Great. Now what?

We looked downriver. Green banks stretched as far as you could see. Here and there, cottonwoods clumped along the shore.

Then, I spotted them. A young human couple,

lounging on a blanket. I could smell the picnic they were having. *Mmm,* chicken salad. On toast—which was what we'd be if they saw Rita.

"Humans—hide!"

Rita crouched out of sight. Together we peered through the cattails. The humans had a little canoe shoved up on the sand by some brush. It was down-river from where they were sitting. But they were be-tween us and it.

"Quackers?" Rita hissed.

"Yup?" he said, paddling over to us.

"Think you can get those two to look at you?"

Quackers looked doubtful. "Them there? What should I do?"

"You want to be in showbiz, right?" she asked. He nodded eagerly. "Well, now's your chance. Give 'em a preview of coming attractions. I don't care if you sing 'The Star-Spangled Banner'! Just get them to look at you, not at that boat!"

Quackers, thrilled with this mission, swam off to-ward the people.

"Up for a cruise, Pete, ol' pal?" Rita asked. Before I could answer, she was on the move. Following Rita's lead, I scurried along the ridge behind the humans.

A frightened squeal from the picnickers made me look over to where they'd been sitting. They weren't sitting anymore. Quackers had waded out of the water, smack up onto their blanket. As if that wasn't enough, he had gone into his dance routine. Spinning and leaping, he was driving them away from the water a step at a time.

No worries about them noticing us now. Quackers was an amateur, but he knew how to hold his audience. They were riveted.

Rita, wasting no time, was already shoving the canoe into the water.

"Isn't this stealing?" I asked.

"Borrowing. We're not gonna keep it." She saw the look in my eye and went on. "What? Can you spring for a couple of plane tickets? Got your credit card?"

What could I say? Like a broken clock, even Rita's right twice a day.

"Don't just stand there. Pull!" Rita ordered.

I pulled. The canoe scratched along a rock, then slipped into the water. And started to float away!

"Get it!" Rita screeched.

Diving off the sandbar, I paddled after the canoe. The current was fairly swift. I could see the tie rope floating behind. I lunged for it, missed, and got a mouthful of water. Lunged again. Got it!

"Rita!" I yelped, mouth full of wet rope. "Help!"

Rita went barreling along the bank ahead of me. Another little sandbar jutted out into the river. She ran to its end and yelled, "Try to steer it this way!"

I dug in as hard as I could. But I was already gasping for breath. I did manage to slow the boat down, though. It eased closer to the bank. Rita crouched, measuring the distance with her eyes. Then gathering herself up, she leaped and landed in the canoe.

Letting go of the rope, I managed to get my paws over the side of the canoe. Rita grabbed hold of me and hauled me in. Both of us went sprawling onto the floor. "Stay down!" I said. "Until we get away."

I peered over the side. There were the picnickers, still being distracted by the daffy duck. Spotting us, Quackers abandoned his act and broke for the water. At that point, the picnickers spotted us, too. But short of running to the bank and yelling, there wasn't much they could do.

Quackers swam up. "Hey, guys—how'd I do?"

Rita grinned, lounging against the seat. "You killed 'em, kid."

Quackers beamed, fluffing his chest out.

I'd never been on a canoe before. Once I got used to the tippy feeling, it was lovely. I rested my nose on the bow, and just watched the world slide by.

The muddy banks seemed to run on and on, like a story with no end. For a while, there were long stretches of nothing but green fields on either side. Here came a sleepy town with a white church steeple like a finger pointed at the sky. Above it, fancy mansions perched on the bluffs. Humble homes huddled down below.

A dragonfly zoomed up to us for a look-see. Rita ducked, then lunged to catch it. The canoe rocked like a cradle. A rusting garbage barge idled by. It left a steamy cloud of stink floating behind it.

"Pete? I'm sorry."

I looked at Rita, surprised. "Whoa. Thought that was the barge. Must have been the apples."

"Not the smell, you dope." She shrugged up one

shoulder, wrinkling her nose. "For messing up the routine. For upstaging you. I'm sorry. It was unprofessional."

"About time you admitted it! Not to mention you got me in trouble . . ."

"Hello? It wasn't me that bit the ringmaster!"

"Which never would have happened, if you hadn't—"

"Hey, are you guys fightin'?"

We'd forgotten about Quackers, who was still cruising alongside.

"No!" Rita snapped. "Why don't you keep your big beak out of it?!"

Quackers retreated, confused. "Sorry. I just thought you was fightin'."

"Well, we're not!" I growled. "We're making up!"

"Funny way to go at it," Quackers muttered. He swam off, looking miffed.

"Are we?" Rita asked. "Making up?"

"I guess. For what it's worth, I'm sorry, too. About biting you. I lost it."

"I had it coming, Bone Breath."

"You think they'll quit giving me the Silent Treatment when we get home?"

Rita lay back in the canoe, arms folded under her head. "When we get home? Buddy, they'll bring on the brass band and pass out pink popcorn. After they pick themselves up off the floor, that is."

"You think?"

"Sure! Don't you see? The last anybody in the troupe knows, we got sucked up by a twister. They don't think we're coming back. They think we're dead."

That curled my tail. Dead? How brokenhearted they all must be! Sure, I'd wanted everyone to miss me. But I hadn't meant to make them *that* miserable. My head drooped down to my paws.

Just then, Quackers started honking like crazy. "People! In the water! Coming this way!"

I picked up my head and peered out. A bunch of kids were clustered on a rickety dock. Two boys were in the water. And they were swimming straight for our canoe!

"Hey, there's a dog in it!" one of the kids called excitedly. Yikes! That was me!

I cowered, horrified. "Rita! What should we do?"

That's when Quackers took matters into his own hands—er, wings.

Squawking furiously, he went for the boys, pecking

for all he was worth. And he was worth plenty. The boys yipped as Quackers nipped. One of them shoved him back and fled. Quackers dived at him, hurrying him along with another pinch. Victory!

But the other one was still headed for the boat, and us!

"Pete! Look over the side, and tell me when he's almost here," Rita hissed. She was crouching on the canoe's bottom. What was she up to?

I peeked out again. Here he came, stroke-stroke-stroking his way nearer by the second. "He's gettin' closer!" I yipped. "Closer, closer—I can see his freckles . . . Rita, he's reaching for the boat!"

"*Yiiiii!*"

Rita sprang up with an ear-splitting shriek! Shaking her head and baring her teeth, she wailed like a siren. Whatever ideas that kid had about capturing our canoe, he forgot 'em, pronto. Terrified, he turned and splashed frantically for the shore.

I watched the kids on the dock haul the two boys up out of the water. The second kid was waving his arms excitedly, pointing at us. I flopped down, panting in relief.

"Nice job, Rita!" Quackers said.

"Yeah. I always said you were a real fright," I added.

Rita chuckled, rocking back on her butt. "Lucky for you, partner. I did hear you tell the duck we're partners, didn't I?"

I let my tail wag an answer.

CHAPTER 13

IF WE WANTED to avoid nosy humans, we had to stay clear of the shore, out in the middle of the river. But with no way to steer the canoe, we were at the mercy of every passing breeze and boat.

Then, Rita saw some guys paddling along the opposite bank. They were in skinny yellow boats that looked like rubber bananas. She noticed that when they paddled on one side, their boats turned toward the opposite direction.

She didn't have oars—but she has hands. Rita reached over the left side of the boat, with me weighting the right side, and paddled. It was just enough to push us toward the middle of the river where we were safe from swimmers and snoops. The current was faster out over the deeper water, and it carried Quackers and us along at a nice clip.

The afternoon was hot and made for napping. I woke up with my stomach growling like a grizzly. When you're used to getting your dinner brought to you in a bowl, you don't think much about it. But when you're on your own with no dinner in sight, it's hard to think about anything else.

"I could go for some of those apples right now." I yawned.

Rita stretched, rubbing her head. "Me, too." She squinted at the orange-streaked sky. "It'll be dark enough pretty soon to risk hitting a town. If you're game."

"I'm game."

The moon was just making her entrance when a likely looking town floated into view on the far bank.

Plunging into the river, I grabbed the rope in my teeth and paddled as hard as I could toward shore. Rita hung over the side and rowed with her hands. With her shoving and me hauling, we were able to get our boat beached. Rita plucked some branches off a bush and spread them over the canoe. Good enough camouflage, if you didn't look too close.

We left Quackers to stand guard. He got busy diving for minnows in the shallows. Rita and I crept up the brushy bank to scout the situation. A dusky haze hung over us. Perfect sneaking-around weather.

The town was a smallish burg, the kind of place our circus plays. The main street ran right down to the river and the little park where we'd landed. The buildings down by the waterfront were mostly brick. A lot of them still had lights on. We could see people strolling, hear them laugh. A kid sped by on his bike, no doubt late for dinner.

A miniature collie with a man on a leash trotted into the park, sniffing around. Suddenly he scented us and started yapping his head off, yanking at his leash.

"My park!" he yipped. "This is my park!" He had a nasty little bark and manners to match. I'd met this kind of townie mutt before. I hadn't liked that one, either.

"Pipe down, Killer," I growled, just loud enough for him to hear me. "We're only passin' through." If he was looking for a dogfight, I wouldn't turn tail. Still, I couldn't risk his human spotting Rita.

My tone clued the collie that I meant business. He pranced away, tugging his human after him. The coast was clear. Rita and I slithered out of the bushes. I put my nose in the air and inhaled.

"Follow me, and keep in the shadows."

I tore across the grass and made for the dark refuge of an alley. Rita stayed on my tail. We scurried up the alley, then down a side street. Rita kept low, all four hands on the ground. From a distance, a human might mistake her for a really ugly dog. But we couldn't count on it.

So we stuck to the walls like shadows. A cat rooting through a garbage can turned to give us the evil eye. I took a good gander at its tail before I growled. No more polecats for me.

He hissed in return—then got a load of Rita. His back rose into a question mark, and he yowled like a second-rate soprano. Rita bared her teeth. The cat shot off like a bullet.

"Think that's worth a dive?" Rita asked, eyeing the can hungrily.

But a more toothsome perfume was calling. "Later, maybe. Right now, I'm hunting burgers."

I trotted up another street, with too many lights for comfort. Rita followed, grumbling. We rounded the corner.

Eureka! There it was, a squat little building lit up like the Fourth of July. A line of cars waited their turn at the drive-thru window. The big rainbow sign promised a pot of gold. I'd have settled for a bag of fries.

Now, how to get them?

We watched as a car pulled up. We could see the driver handing money to a kid inside the window. The kid reached out and passed the driver a whopping white paper bag. I could smell it from across the street.

"Look! That's where the food comes out," I hissed to Rita. "There's no way we can . . ."

Zzzip, Rita was gone! Faster than a flea, she was across the street, skirting the shadowy edge of the parking lot. She came to an old maple tree, its branches spreading wide over the roof. A leap, a rustle, and she was up in its leafy canopy. Now what?

I watched, frozen, as Rita dropped onto the roof and disappeared. Forgetting all about lying low, I ran up to the joint, barking.

"Rita! Are you okay?"

"Pipe down!" she hissed. "Go over by where the cars pull up. When you see a really big order coming out, make some noise."

I trotted over as a second car pulled up. This one only had a couple of humans in it. The lady sitting on the passenger side saw me watching. When their bag was handed out to them, she threw me a fry. I gobbled it down gratefully.

"Hey!" That was Rita, on the roof.

"Sorry!" I whined. "But it was real small."

"Just stick with the routine!" she snapped.

Ha! Where had I heard *that* before.

Next in line was a minivan full of yelling girls in softball uniforms. The dazed-looking dad at the wheel passed the guy in the window a big wad of bills. To my delight, he grabbed two humongous bags of food. I could see they were heavy. The dad had to lean way out to grab them—

"Rita!" I barked. "Now!" And I started throwing flips and yipping at the top of my lungs.

Voilà! The girls plastered their noses to the windows to watch me. The dad froze in surprise, those tempting bags of goodies dangling halfway between van and building. Right on cue, here came Rita! She dropped off the roof and snatched the sacks.

The dad yelped like a seal and jerked his hands

back. The girls in the van started screaming and pointing at Rita, who was making her escape, a bag under each arm. She was halfway down the block before I remembered to follow.

I heard the van doors open and looked over my shoulder. Horrors! The team was piling out. I could hear the dad yelling at them to get back in the car. But they were already giving chase. And they were gaining!

"Rita! Hustle!"

Rita looked back, saw the girls coming, and stepped on the gas. But those bulky bags were weighing her down.

I caught up to her. "We gotta lose them!" I yipped. "Follow me." I snatched one of the bags from her and cut left into a side street.

I could hear the girls clattering after us in their cleats. As we passed under a streetlight, I heard one cry out, "There they are!"

Yikes! We zoomed into the alley. Rita grabbed me, dragging me behind a pile of crates. A split second later the team thundered by. Safe!

We wasted no time getting back to the park and under the cover of the bushes.

"That was definitely stealing!" I panted.

Rita tossed me a burger. "No. That's entertainment. People pay to see you perform, right? Mike buys your food with the money. We just cut out the middleman."

That chimp could tie the truth into a pretzel.

But what could I do? I ate. And ate. Those kids must have ordered one of everything on the menu. By the time I'd munched my way through the triple bacon barbecue burger, I was fit to bust.

We managed to waddle down to the river. Quackers had his head under his wing, bagging z's.

"Some watch duck," Rita griped. But when we got closer Quackers startled into action. Honking and flapping, he charged at us, then skidded to a stop.

"'Bout time! I was gettin' sleepy."

Together we pulled the brush off of the canoe. Grunting, Rita shoved it over the sticky mud back into the river. Quackers plopped into the bow and went right back to sleep. I took a running jump from the bank and made it into the stern. Rita leaped and managed to land on top of me. We were on our way.

There's nothing like a full belly to bring on a nap. I sprawled on my back, paws up. It was heaven. The evening was warm. The mists had cleared, and the stars were making their entrance. They looked like sequin sparkles dancing on the roof of our circus tent. Whirling and swirling . . . Gee, I could almost hear the music . . .

Huh!? I *could* hear the music!

My eyelids flew up like window shades, and I lifted my head. The fur on the back of my neck was tingling. The music was getting louder. *Boom! Boom!* Either somebody was beating the world's biggest base drum, or—

"Pete?" I heard Rita mutter, still half asleep. "Whuz-zaht?"

Suddenly Quackers was shrieking the alarm. "Dive! Dive!"

We didn't wait to ask questions. Rita flew off one side. Quackers and I tumbled over the other. A second later, a steamboat the size of Texas plowed through the canoe, turning it into toothpicks.

CHAPTER 14

I **DIVED DEEP** and stayed down as long as I could. The wheel of the steamboat was churning the water so hard it was like riding the tornado all over again. I felt like a sock in the spin cycle.

Finally, I couldn't stand it anymore. I had to breathe or bust!

I broke the surface, gasping. The steamboat was already way downriver. The word CASINO twinkled in lights on its stern. I could still hear the music, fainter now. A chunk of the canoe floated by. I leaned my paws on it and tried to catch my breath.

Rita bobbed up next to me like a cork. She grabbed for the floating board, too, and we hung on to it together.

Quackers was already at the water's edge, thrashing around in a panic. "Pete! Rita! Are you guys dead?"

"Not yet, my feathered friend," I barked back. "Many thanks to you."

Clinging to our life raft, Rita and I kicked slowly to the shore and waded out. I flopped onto the mud, exhausted. Rita sprawled next to me. Quackers settled close by and ruffled his feathers, his little black eyes dancing. Now that the danger was past, he looked downright tickled.

"Ever since I met you two, my life has really opened up. Know what I mean? Leavin' the farm, seein' the world? Out here on the river, havin' us a time. Big ol' boat come along, and *kabam!*" He chuckled. "You circus folk sure know how to have fun."

"Fun?" Rita lifted her head off the mud and glared at him. "You call getting run over by a steamboat fun? Traveling night and day, fun? Not knowing whether you're gonna get the royal treatment or run out of town, *fun?*" She moaned and let her head flop down again. "Pete, are you thinking what I'm thinking?"

"Yup. He's perfect for show business."

Quackers stared at us, beak hanging open. "You kidding me, ain'cha?"

I sat up and shook my head. "Anybody crazy enough to think he's having a good time on this escapade belongs in the circus. Right, Rita?"

"Only place for him," she agreed.

"You guys mean it? Really? You'll take me back to the circus with you?" Quackers squeaked, trembling.

"You keep saving our lives. It's getting embarrassing. Besides, a duck might really freshen up our act."

"But no impressions!" Rita warned. "We'll come up with something."

"Sure, sure!" Quackers fluttered. "Whatever you say! Wow! If Mama could see me now. Yeehaw!" And he went into a mad dance of joy.

Rita looked at me and shrugged. "Definitely nuts. But he's growing on me."

I nodded. Skills, you can learn. But heart? That, you've got to be born with. It's what gets you past a tough audience or a bad break. Even a tornado. Quackers was short on skills but long on heart. He'd get his shot at showbiz.

Now all we had to do was travel a couple thousand more miles. On foot. And keep from starving, getting captured, or just plain killed on the way.

The river, which had been wide before, was twice as big across here. We'd washed up on the banks of a city. Cities meant people, lots of them. We needed to get on the move. But where to? The buildings stretched as far as I could see in all directions. We were surrounded.

Rita read my mind. "We're sitting ducks out here," she said. "No pun intended. We'll have to find a place to hide before it gets light." I didn't want to ask her what we'd do then. I was pretty sure she didn't know, either.

"This time I'm comin', too," Quackers quacked. "You guys might need me."

As we were talking, one of those thick, low fogs eased in. Its tendrils seemed to wrap around us as we edged up the banks. There was a narrow yellow-hued ribbon of brick, running alongside the river. It was wide enough for people to walk on and edged with patches of grass.

A wadded-up brown bag blew by. I sniffed it. Salami sandwich. Chocolate cookie. Yum. Somebody's lunch had been in that bag not more than a day ago.

"I think the people in those big buildings must come out here to eat," I offered. "Maybe we should hang around, work the crowd for a handout. I'd rather sing for my supper than snatch it."

"The only thing they'll hand me is a trip to the zoo." Rita sniffed. "Let's find a tree where I can hide. Then you can do your stuff."

The fog was plenty thick by now. The sky was starting to glow with dawn's early light. "Which way should we go?" Quackers asked.

Rita squinted into the distance. "I think I see some big trees down that way. Plus, if we stay close to the water, we know we're still headed south. Right, Quackers?"

"Rightaroony, Rita."

"So, we should . . . follow the yellow brick road?" I asked.

"Yep. Follow the yellow brick road."

I stifled a sudden urge to skip. Weird.

We went on our way, sticking close to the shrubbery on the riverside. If any early-bird joggers came along, we had to be able to pull a disappearing act, and fast.

Suddenly, out of the fog came a rough voice. A man's voice!

"Freeze! We got you covered!"

CHAPTER 15

WE FROZE. Quackers cowered behind Rita, who was trying to hide behind me.

A second voice piped up from the other side of the road. A woman!

"Hey, sailor! Fleet's in!"

Huh!? Sure, we'd just gotten off a boat. But only a nut would mistake us for sailors. Zounds! Were we surrounded by crazies? My heart beat so hard I was sure they could hear it.

A third voice froze me to the marrow.

"Pretty bird! Pretty bird!"

Quackers moaned in terror. Rita went ape.

Baring her impressive teeth, she jumped up and

down, making low, furious grunts. The effect was amazing. Even I was scared of her! Then she gave out an ear-stabbing bellow that would panic a banshee.

That started up a chorus of answering screeches so shrill it made my teeth ache.

"What the . . . ?" Rita clamped her hands over her ears. For once, I wished I had hands.

Wings flapped in the darkness. Something fluttered past my head with an angry squawk.

We looked around wildly. Where were they? *What* were they?

"Up there! Birds!" Quackers reported. He was peering toward the top of the lamppost. "Looks like some of them's tangled in a net or somethin'."

Rita and I followed his gaze.

"Yeah, I see 'em. It looks like they're trapped," I said.

Rita raised her eyebrows. "Who'd want to trap birds?"

"You could ask 'em yourself. You could climb right up there, couldn't ya? You could let 'em go!" Quackers looked hopefully at Rita, then at me.

Rita sighed. None of us animals like the idea of

traps. It's one of those human things that we just don't get. Helping the birds would be the right thing to do.

But what if the trap caught Rita?

I could tell she was thinking the same thing. Why should she risk her neck for strangers? Neither of us could look Quackers in the eye. Still, there was no nice way to say "no."

Quackers took that for a "yes." Craning his neck up, he squawked, "Hang on, y'all! Rita's comin' to save the day!" He beamed at Rita, settling his wings.

For a moment, I thought she was going to take a poke at him. Instead, she turned to glare at me.

"What?" I protested. "I didn't say anything!"

"I noticed!" she spat. Grumbling to herself, Rita wrapped both sets of nimble fingers around the lamp-post and scooted up.

Quackers and I waited. There she was, nearly at the top. The birds were flying around her, shrieking. Were they trying to scare her off? I could hear Rita chittering something, and them chattering back. But I couldn't make out what they were saying. I held my breath until Rita called down to us.

"It's okay! I got 'em loose."

Rita slid down the post. A big-beaked military macaw was perched on her shoulder.

"Boys, this is El Jefe. He's boss bird of that bunch on the light post."

"Libertad, mis hijos!" squawked the macaw. I noticed he was missing an eye. The crinkled black skin that covered it looked like an eye patch.

"Er—Liberace to you, too, pal." I wasn't sure what that meant, but I wanted to be polite. "Everything okay up there?"

El Jefe leaned toward me, fixing me with a one-eyed, bug-eyed stare. *"Si, hermano,* thanks to your monkey."

I choked. "Not *my* monkey, pal."

"I'm no monkey, you overstuffed parakeet!" Rita snapped. If there's one thing Rita hates, it's being called a monkey.

Suddenly, the air was full of birds. Green, red, gold—a rainbow of birds, fluttering down and settling all around us.

"What—what are you guys?" Quackers quavered.

El Jefe, still perched on Rita, looked around at the others. "Tell them, *mis hijos!*"

So they stretched their necks and sang. Everybody seemed to have a different idea of the tune. But the words were pretty good.

Hey-yo, hey-o, a parrot's life for me!
No cage is home, we soar and roam
The city bold and free!
We fly as we please, we nest in the trees,
We ride on the wind and float on the breeze,
And no man's pet we'll be.
A parrot's life for me!

"Very nice," I offered. "I especially like the 'nest in trees' bit. Though it looks like a lamppost from here."

El Jefe nodded his head. "*Sí*, that's the trouble. The humming beans don't like our kind." He turned to the other birds and hollered, "Do they, *amigos*?" The birds clucked angrily.

I'd heard of lima beans and green beans. But humming beans?

"I think he means 'human beings,'" Rita whispered.

"Whatever! The enemy!" El Jefe snapped. Rita flinched.

El Jefe was just warming up. He hopped off her

shoulder and paced back and forth. The other birds crowded closer, muttering.

"To a humming bean, the only good bird is a caged bird! But we'd sooner starve, wouldn't we, *hermanos*?" This got a raucous squawk of approval. "So they set their snapper-trappers, and their dangly-tanglys, and their Polly wanna crackers? Preetty bird! Preetty bird! Iddy widdy coo? Iddy widdy coo?" A glazed look came over his bulgy eye. "Coo? Coo?"

Rita sneaked an alarmed glance at me.

"Come again?" I asked.

A little green lorikeet hurried up. "Don't mind him," she whispered. "It's Old Pet's Syndrome. See, El Jefe used to belong to a humming bean. She taught him to talk. Once a parrot learns a thing, it stays with him forever."

At that, El Jefe burst into "Lady of Spain" in a shaky soprano, swaying to the beat.

The lorikeet leaned over to El Jefe and pecked him hard on the head. El Jefe shuddered and quit singing.

"*Gracias*, Dolores," he wheezed. "I needed that." He turned to us. "What brings you here?"

"We're just passing through. We need a place to hide," Rita said. "A place with trees."

"And water!" Quackers added.

"And food!" That was my stomach talking.

El Jefe nodded up the road. "Straight ahead. We will take you there. But beware. It will be crawling with humming beans soon."

Circling and swooping, the wild parrots guided us up the yellow brick road. We got to enjoy another chorus of their freedom song along the way. Catchy. Quackers joined in on the last "hey-yos."

In a few minutes, we were at the edge of the park. There was a cluster of tall trees, some shrubbery, and a nice little pond. Perfect!

El Jefe lit on the back of a bench and turned to Rita. "We free ones owe you a debt of honor, Monkey. And we never forget."

I saw Rita flinch at "monkey," but she let it go.

"If you're ever in a tight spot, sound the cry *'Libertad!'* The free ones will fly to your aid. *Es verdad, mis hijos?*" A happy twittering from his buddies was the answer.

I could have used a lot of things just then. My cozy boxcar, a sack of kibble, and a good brushing. But help from a bunch of birds? I had to hide a grin.

We said our good-byes.

"Fly safe, *amigos!*" El Jefe called out. "Beware the humming beans!"

The flock lifted with a whirr of wings. In moments, they were just a fast-moving cloud against the sky. Their cries faded in the distance.

Rita cracked her knuckles, then shinnied up a handy tree. To my horror, she pulled a twig off of it and actually nibbled on the leaves!

"Stop! Have you gone nuts? You can't eat that! It's not even food!" I yelped.

She wrinkled her nose, but ate another leaf. "I know this seems odd. But it's not bad." She snapped off another twig and started stripping it. Ugh!

"Instinct. That's what that is," Quackers said wisely.

I shuddered. What was happening to us? Rita eating leaves and liking it? Curling up in a tree to sleep like it was normal? She was going wild, right before my very eyes. Would I start to go wild, too? I didn't even know how! I had a feeling it involved eating some pretty disgusting things. And running with a herd, or a pack, or whatever.

We had to get home, before Nature got the better of us. Tomorrow we'd be on our way as soon as it was safe.

But this had been a trying night, and I was dog tired. Quackers and I stole into a bush underneath the tree and went straight to Dreamland.

CHAPTER 16

THE SUN WAS HIGH when I awoke. I yawned and stretched. There was my stomach, sounding off again. The rumbling woke Quackers, who fluffed his feathers. We wriggled out into the open.

It was a nice little city park, built around a big circle of grass. There were benches, vendors, a few kids, and a lot of business types sauntering through. Lunchtime. No wonder I was hungry.

The park had a pond, and Quackers hopped right in. If a duck could smile, he'd have been grinning ear to ear. A group of local ducks were gathered around a little boy with a bag of stale bread. Quackers paddled over to join them.

Rita was safe in the tree. All I had to do was find some chow. But how?

I checked out the park. A man with a hot dog stand was lifting the lid to the cooker. Clouds of heavenly hot-doggy steam wafted my way.

I crept closer, trying to look hungry and pathetic. It wasn't hard. He cut me a nasty look and kicked side-ways at me.

"Shoo!" he hissed, flourishing his big fork like a spear. I backed off. Not an animal lover. I looked around. A nice-looking young woman in a black suit was perched on a bench, eating a sandwich. She saw me looking and smiled. Tearing off a chunk of her sandwich, she threw it toward me. Gratefully, I jumped for it.

Not fast enough. A flock of pushy pigeons beat me to it. By the time I'd scattered them, there wasn't a crumb left. I looked at the woman hopefully.

She shrugged, holding up the empty bag. "Sorry, doggy. All gone."

Doggone.

Now what? The lunchtime crowd was beginning to thin out. I spotted a little gaggle of people at the other edge of the park gathered to watch something. What?

I nosed my way through the forest of legs.

A skinny young guy in tattered jeans and a tie-dyed shirt stood on a threadbare blanket. He had a baggy striped cap with long fuzzy braids sticking out of it. A jaunty gold hoop glittered in his ear.

And he was juggling.

Or trying to. He had three skinny sticks wrapped in bright-colored tape, with tassels on the ends. The idea was to hold one of them in each hand and toss the third back and forth. But every time he tried, he'd drop one. His battered tip cup held a lonely dollar bill. The way he juggled, George Washington wasn't going to get any company.

Ouch! He hit himself in the head. That got a laugh, and not the kind you like to hear. The onlookers were starting to fall away. This act was going down in flames.

As a performer, I knew the feeling. Without thinking, I jumped in to save him. Or rather, I danced in, up on my hind legs. Just as he dropped another juggling stick, I caught it in my teeth. Before he could grab it back, I started twirling it! Around and around his blanket I went, spinning that stick in my teeth. The audience burst into applause. The guy just stood there, flabbergasted.

I tossed the stick into the air, then caught it on my nose. I flipped it high, rolled over, then hopped to my feet in time to catch it again!

Applause, applause! The tip cup was suddenly overflowing. The guy stumbled through some thank-yous and quickly stuffed the money into his jeans. I stood there, tail wagging. He bent down and gave me a pat.

"Pretty fancy footwork, dude. What'd you do? Fall from the sky?" he asked. Oh, how right he was! He felt around my neck for a collar, but there wasn't one. "Guess I owe you a piece of the profits. How 'bout we do lunch?"

Reaching into his pocket, he walked over to the hot dog stand and came back with two franks. He set mine on the ground. I bolted it down.

"Feeding strays, Jimmy? What are you, nuts?" A beefy bowlegged guy with a jaw like a bulldog was glaring down at me. My new best friend finished his lunch.

"Dude, he earned it. You shoulda seen this pup. He juggles better than me!"

"That wouldn't take much!" The beefy guy took off his glasses and cleaned them on his T-shirt. I could see where he'd stuck them together with a wad of dirty tape in the middle. He jammed them back on his face and eyeballed me. "Show me."

Jimmy waved one of the sticks at me. "Here, boy." He tossed it up. I jumped onto my hind legs and caught it. Before the beefy guy could make a crack, I started twirling the stick in my mouth. I jerked my head, throwing the stick up and catching it. A mother with a couple of tired-looking kids slowed down to watch. The kids quit whining and clapped their hands in delight.

"Mama, goggy wiv a stick!" the littler boy gurgled. The mom reached into her purse and pulled out a wad of dollar bills. She thrust them at Jimmy.

"That's the first time they've stopped crying in an hour!" She and the kids moved on. Jimmy waved the money at his pal, grinning.

"See, Gerry? What'd I tell ya? This puppy's an earner."

Gerry nodded, scratching his head. A flurry of dandruff fell. *Yuck.* This guy needed a groomer worse than I did.

Plus, I didn't care for the way he was looking at me. It was the same way I'd looked at my hot dog.

"We could use an earner. Until the 'thing' comes through."

Jimmy brightened, like Gerry had just given him a present. "Can we keep him, Ger? Can we?"

Gerry rolled his eyes. "Yeah, yeah. As long as he's bringing in bucks. 'Cause you sure ain't."

Jimmy rolled up his rug and slung it over his shoulder. He stuffed the juggling sticks into his backpack. "You're not bringing in so much, either," Jimmy said under his breath. Gerry glared at him, then started counting the money we'd collected.

"I'm the one who thought up the business plan. Remember?

Jimmy brightened. "Right! And we're gonna start a—what d'you call it?"

"A franchise, Jimster. Deep-fried pizza on a stick. Gonna be the biggest thing to hit the snack-food world since toaster pastries."

"Every kid in America will be stuffin' 'em down. Our pictures will be right on the wrapper. Right, Ger? And we don't even gotta get our hands dirty. Just count the money."

"That's right, Jimster. We just gotta wait for the big score. Which will be any day now. Let's go."

He started off, then stopped, looking at me again. "You bringing the dog?"

Jimmy squatted down, backpack in hand. "Come on, boy. Come home with us. Lots of hot dogs!"

He seemed like a nice guy. But Gerry didn't. And I couldn't leave Rita and Quackers. I was giving Jimmy's hand a friendly good-bye lick, when he suddenly slipped a loop of rope around my neck!

I jerked my head back, surprised, and the rope tightened. A choke knot! Jimmy leered at the look on my face. Suddenly, he didn't seem like a nice guy at all. He stood up, the end of the rope wrapped tight around his fist.

I felt like a prize chump, getting suckered like that. I snarled. Jimmy jerked the rope hard enough to gag me. Then he pulled harder. I had to go with him or give up breathing. Not much of a choice. But how to warn Rita?

As we passed under the tree where Rita was hiding, I darted to the other side, wrapping the rope around the trunk. Jimmy had to walk around to unwrap it. So I took the moment to yip,

"Stay up there! Don't try anything! These guys are bad news."

"Don't worry, Pete. I'll find you . . ." she hissed. Jimmy must have heard her because he stopped pulling to peer up into the tree.

"What was that?" he asked.

Oh, no! If they were mean enough to choke a poor performing poodle, what might they do to a chimp? I started frisking around, barking, trying to distract him. But he didn't pay me any mind.

"Rita! Hide!" I yelped, frantic. I heard a soft rustle in the branches as she climbed higher.

Unfortunately, Jimmy heard it, too. "Gerry, come over here. There's something up this tree!" he called.

CHAPTER 17

IN ALL THE excitement, I'd forgotten Quackers. But he hadn't forgotten us.

Squawking up a storm, Quackers came barreling out of the pond. He jumped at Jimmy, clamping his beak on my captor's baby finger. Jimmy went nuts, flailing and yelling, trying to knock him off. But ol' Quackers was made of tougher stuff.

It wasn't until Gerry grabbed him by the feet and pulled that he let go. Even that didn't break his fighting spirit. When Gerry swung a kick at him, Quackers took a snap at his ankle. From the way Gerry yelped, I think Quackers got some skin.

"Crazy duck!" Jimmy whined, sucking his dented digit. Gerry was hopping on one leg and saying things

I wouldn't quote, even if I knew how to spell them. A stern voice made us all look around.

"Hey! No harassing the ducks!" A cop stood glaring at us.

Jimmy popped his finger out of his mouth and waved it at the cop. "He was harassing *us*!"

The cop eyed me. "You got a license for that dog?"

Gerry slid in, slick as oil. "We were just on our way to City Hall to get one, Officer." He smiled. "We're with the Poodle Rescue Society. This poor little doggie was abandoned. Can you imagine?"

I tried to bark a warning, but Jimmy jerked the rope tight.

"Well, take him and go, then. Just leave the ducks alone."

"You got it!" Jimmy snapped. He jerked again at the rope. "Come on, doggie."

I went. What else could I do? At least they'd forgotten about the Mystery Animal in the tree. Quackers darted out from behind the cop's legs as we passed.

"Pete! Should I bite him again?"

"No! Stay in the pond and wait. I'll shake these guys and come back for you!" I managed to say. Quackers snapped me a salute and waddled away.

Gerry started off, Jimmy and me behind him. Jimmy was rougher with the rope than he needed to be, just out of spite. He kept sucking his sore finger, which was turning the color of an eggplant, and cutting me dirty looks.

My new best friend—yeesh. I remembered what Mom used to say. Beware of strangers passing out treats. Even really good ones.

We walked through the crowds around the lofty, glittering office buildings. As we traveled, I noticed that the streets got narrower. The buildings were smaller in this part of town and not so clean. Fewer people were out walking. Battered garbage cans leaned against each other, overflowing. There weren't so many cars here and no taxis.

I tried to memorize the way we were going, in case I could break free. But the streets had gotten all twisty. Could I find my way back to the park? I wasn't sure. The farther we went, the less sure I felt.

Where were we going, anyway?

We came to a grimy apartment building. Gerry shouldered through the front door and led us up five flights of echoing stairs. Then down a hallway that stunk of cabbage and cat. A single bulb flickered overhead. I'd always wondered what these places were like inside. This one made my old boxcar seem like a palace.

Their apartment was at the end of the hall. Gerry fished out a key ring and undid three locks. Before he opened the door, he checked over both shoulders. Once we were in, Gerry locked it behind us. I wondered why there were so many locks on a dump like this. There wasn't much to steal. A few forlorn pieces of furniture. A stack of pizza boxes on the coffee table. A tiny TV flickered silently.

"The news!" Gerry hurried over to the TV. Jimmy pulled off his hat. To my surprise, the frizzy braids came off with it! Underneath, he was as bald as an egg. *Hmm*. A costume? Or . . . a disguise?

On the television, the news guy was in front of a photo of the Airhead Heiress and her missing dog. Gerry was trying to turn it up, but there was something wrong with the sound.

"Smack it!" Jimmy suggested.

Gerry glared at him. "How about I smack you instead?"

Jimmy was so interested in what was on the screen that he dropped the rope—the one that was around my neck. The knot loosened a little. I peeked at Gerry. Ha! He was still messing with the TV. Now was my chance!

Moving as quietly as possible, I slunk behind the sofa and looked around. I could smell fresh air blowing in from the next room. An open window?

I stole into the kitchen. There it was! The window was propped up with a stick. There wasn't more than a foot of space, but I'd gotten through tighter spots. The only problem was how to get down without breaking my neck. That first step would be a doozy.

I put my paws on the sill and peered out. Aha! A rusty fire escape, just outside. I glanced back over my shoulder. It was now or never.

With an effort, I heaved one back leg up onto the sill and shoved my shoulders through the narrow opening. Hind legs scrabbling, I tried to worm my belly through. Freedom was a paw's-length away! I could feel its sweet breath on my muzzle.

Just then, the rope around my neck went tight! I was being hauled back through the window. There was Jimmy, bald head gleaming, grinning at me. I fell in a heap on the floor, choking.

"Nice try, mutt!" Jimmy sneered, jerking me to my feet. "You've got a time out comin'." With that, he dragged me down the hall to a padlocked bedroom door. I struggled to get the rope in my teeth as he fumbled with the key. Jimmy got the lock off and, with a mighty kick, sent me tumbling into the shuttered room. The door slammed behind me. I heard the click of the padlock and Jimmy's retreating footsteps.

Groaning, I got to my feet. My eyes adjusted to the darkness. I saw that I wasn't alone.

There before me, shivering in terror, was a rat. A really *big* rat. With bulgy eyes. And a dirty pink angora sweater. I could see a name embroidered on it.

BABY.

CHAPTER 18

YOU BETTUH BE HEAH to wescue me!" the rat—
er, Baby—squeaked. She sounded like an angry
rubber ducky.

Finally, I remembered my manners.

"Pierre Le Chien, at your service. You can call me
Pete."

"Well, it's about time! For stahters, you can get me
something decent to eat! Then winse out this sweatah.
It's totally gwoss. And I need my nails clipped. Wight
now!"

"Uh—Miss?" I interrupted. Clearly she had mistaken
me for the maid. "I regret that I am unable to . . ."

"Don't call me 'Miss'! That's Mistuh Baby to you."

Oooh, awkward. "A thousand pardons, sir—the sweater . . ."

"You think I dwess myself?! Please!" Baby flopped on the floor. "Pink, pink, pink—it's like an obsession with heh. I'd like a nice houndstooth check or maybe a pinstwipe for a change. But no. It's always this cwummy pink."

"I'm usually pink myself. But I'm between dye jobs," I offered. Baby blinked at me, surprised. "I'm with Circus Martinez. You've heard of it?"

"Ciwcus? What would dognappuhs want with a tacky ciwcus dog?" Baby sniffed.

Tacky? *Moi?*

Baby was getting on my nerves.

"For your four-one-one, *Mister* Baby, you're talking to a headliner. Formerly top dog in Monsieur Moliere's Performing Pups. I'm the 'Pete' in 'Pete and Rita,' and we're the biggest thing on the bill."

Baby rolled his bulgy eyes. "Weally? Then what awe you doing hewe?"

What, indeed?

"Long tale short? I had this crazy idea it'd be nice to be . . . well, *you.* A pampered pet. You know. The whole pink feed bowl and silken pillow routine."

Baby stared at me, then gave a gasping whine that turned into a series of hiccups. It took me a moment to realize he was laughing.

"Like me? Awe you cwazy?" He stood up and started pacing back and forth. "Let me tell you a thing oh two about being a pampehed pet! Dwagged fwom pillah to post. Always being cawwied. Dwessed like a doll. Even my name—Baby! It's humiliating. She tweets me like an—an accessowwy, not an animal! She never even pets me, unless theh's a photogwapher awound. The only one who eveh walked me was Quinn, the maid. I thought she was my fwiend, but she . . ." At this, Baby threw back his head and howled.

"She what?" I asked.

"She betwayed me! She handed me ovuh to these dognappuhs!" He sniffled.

Aha! An inside job.

"Woof. Sorry, pal. When humans go bad, it ain't pretty." I filled Baby in on how I'd come to find myself at the end of a rope. Baby gawked at me, amazed.

"You can weally do all that? Juggle and stuff? How'd you luhn?"

"My humans taught me."

He thought about that as he scratched his ear.

"Youh humans? Do they pet you? Or give you tweets?"

"Well, of course. They love us. We're family."

Baby's ears drooped. "I wish I had a family."

"Your heiress will be so glad to see you, she'll pet you all the time."

"Lacie? Nah. All she cahes about is getting heh pictuh in the papehs. I'm just a pwop. I might as well be stuffed."

What could I say? I rolled onto my back to squash a pesky flea. I'd been a working dog ever since I was a pup. Showbiz is a tough racket. Training, rehearsals, matinees, and night shows. Always on the move.

Compared to that, Baby's life of leisure suddenly seemed like a prison. What good was a pink feed bowl, if you hadn't worked up an honest appetite? Or a silken pillow, if you weren't tired from a good day's work? I rolled over and sat up.

"Look, Baby. I don't know how, but I'm gonna get out of this dump. And I'll spring you, too. I got friends on the outside. They'll come for me." Just saying that made me feel better.

Baby wagged his stubby tail hopefully. "Fwiends? Do they know wheh you awe?"

"No." Suddenly I felt worse again.

Baby's tail stopped. "Oh, deah. Unless they'uh blood-hounds, I'm afwaid you and me are in the same boat."

Hmm. My luck with boats hadn't been too good. Then I had a sudden comforting thought.

"Once the ransom is paid, these guys will be only too glad to get you back to the Airhead—er, Miss Whyte. After all, they want money, not pets, right? They won't need a performing poodle, either. So even if we can't escape, we'll be okay."

Just then, a hubbub started out in the hall. A woman's voice rose angrily.

"What are you, nuts? Puttin' Baby in with some dog off the street? What if it eats him? You think of that, Mister Deep Fried Pizza?"

"On a stick," Jimmy grumbled. "You forgot the stick."

There was a clatter as someone fumbled to get the key in the lock. The door swung open with a bang. There stood a young woman, hands on her hips. She glared at me, then at Baby cowering in the corner. She'd have been a knockout as far as humans go, if she hadn't looked so blazing mad.

"It's Quinn—the maid! Pwotect me!" Baby whined, quivering like a Jell-O mold.

I squared my shoulders and looked Quinn right in the eye. I gave her a gander of my canines and a *gr-r-r-r* to go with it. She backed up a step.

"See? What'd I tell ya? He's vicious!" she snapped over her shoulder. Behind her, Gerry and Jimmy peered in.

"Baby looks okay to me," Jimmy said. "I think *you're* the scary one, Quinn."

Quinn rounded on Jimmy and gave him a clout on the head. "Why would he be scared of me, dimwit?" Jimmy backed off, looking hurt.

"Mama always said you were mean." He pouted.

Mama? These two were littermates?

Quinn's eyes became angry slits. She shoved her face so close to Jimmy's they practically rubbed noses.

"Mean? If it wasn't for me, you two would still be running granny games for chump change. I'm the one giving you a shot at the big time. Just remember that. And try not to mess it up!"

My ears pricked up. I'd heard this kind of thieves' lingo before. Our circus had played at some small-town fairs. This bunch talked like the lowlife carnies that ran the crooked games. Swell. Not just dognappers but con artists.

Funny-sounding music started playing in her pocket. Quinn rolled her eyes and dug out a cell phone.

"The Airhead!" she hissed. Then, in a voice sweet enough to make your teeth hurt, she answered. "Yes, Miss Lacie?"

Hot dog! I turned to Baby. "It's your human! Speak!"

Baby leaped to his feet and started barking like crazy. Quinn glared daggers and made a quick throat-cutting motion. She hurried to the door, talking loudly.

"What, Miss Lacie? Oh, no, just some nasty little dog on the street . . . Yes, I ordered the flowers . . ." Bang! The door slammed behind her. But Baby kept barking.

Grabbing a dirty blanket off the floor, Jimmy edged toward Baby.

"Look out!" I yipped. Jimmy tossed the blanket over the poor pup, muffling him. Then he heaved him into the closet like a sack of spuds and slammed the door.

It looked as though Baby's cry for help had

failed. I could hear him throwing himself against the closet door. A valiant effort, but no dice.

"Cool it, Baby," I called. "Your maid friend is gone."

The noise in the closet stopped.

I looked up to see Gerry staring at me. I didn't like it. Suddenly he smiled. I liked that even less.

"You and Baby are real little buddies, aren't you?" he cooed. "Regular new best friends. Well, in a couple of days, you'll be together for good. 'Cause when we collect from the Airhead Heiress? You and Baby are gonna go into a nice big hole in the ground."

A shiver crawled down my back. Gerry laughed.

"Couple of dumb mutts. But maybe not too dumb to lead the cops to us, if we did let you go. Why risk it? We'll already have the money."

My heart turned into a lump of lead. These guys weren't gonna send Baby home to Mama and turn me loose. They were going to steal the ransom, and then . . .

Jimmy stuck his head in the doorway. "Are you talking to that dog?"

Gerry chuckled. "Sure. He's smarter than you."

"Quinn wants you."

Gerry followed Jimmy out, closing the door. I heard the snap of the lock.

"They're gone," I said to the closet door.

"Can you let me out?" Baby called.

"I can twy—er, try." I stood up on my hind legs and pawed the doorknob. "Push!"

Baby pushed. The door swung open. I knew I'd have to tell him what Gerry had planned for us. Unless he'd overheard?

"Uh, Baby . . . ?"

He threw back his head and howled. "We'uh doomed! Dooooomed! Bwaha-ha-haaa!"

Yeah, he'd heard.

CHAPTER 19

BABY WAS SO BLUE he turned up his nose at dinner. "Why botheh?" he whined. "We'uh gonna die!"

My appetite had gone into hiding, too. But I made a big show of chowing down. Then I shoved Baby's feed bowl under his nose.

"You've gotta keep up your strength, Baby. You might need it."

"Fow what? We don't have a hope!"

I shook my head. "Hope's all we do have. These guys aren't the brightest bulbs in the marquee. All we need is for them to make one mistake."

Unfortunately, Jimmy seemed to realize that, too. Or maybe being so close to getting his big payday made him more wary. The next morning, he came in and carefully shut the door behind him. I noticed he was wearing that goofy hat with the braids. His juggling sticks jutted out of the top of his backpack.

Before I knew it, he'd tossed a long, thin steel cord over my head. Urgh! I tried to shake it off, but one hard jerk from Jimmy stopped that.

"Time for a walk, doggy," he said.

Okay. I needed one. Maybe I'd have a chance to make a break for it. Even so, I hated to leave Baby behind. Baby hated it, too. I could hear him howling until we got to the sidewalk outside.

"We're going to the park, and you're gonna earn your keep," Jimmy growled.

My heart leaped! The park! Rita and Quackers would be there. Somehow, they'd free me, and we'd rescue Baby. My tail wagged at the thought.

But wait a minute. This wasn't the way we'd come before! I looked back over my shoulder as Jimmy pulled me down the block. Where was he taking me?

Jimmy had the steel cord wrapped double around his fist. There was no way to break free. All I could do was keep my eyes peeled and wait for him to drop his guard.

The crummy neighborhood gave way to a nicer

one with swanky shops and well-dressed people. Finally, we came to a park. A group of kids dug in a sandbox. Their moms watched from nearby benches. Some college types were standing around sipping take-out coffee. A handful of guys hung over a chess game, while an old lady scattered seed to pigeons from a paper sack.

Jimmy picked a sunny spot by a big fountain. He unrolled his threadbare rug and took out the juggling sticks. He tossed them in the air and dropped one when he tried to catch them. I grinned in spite of myself. This guy was hopeless.

He saw me watching and threw one of the sticks to me. I snagged it easy. Reflexes and a lifetime of training is all it takes. Well, this dog wasn't gonna play today. I dropped the stick and flopped to the ground.

Jimmy glared daggers at me. "Get up!" he hissed, jerking the cord.

I yawned.

He jerked it hard. I grabbed it in my teeth and pulled back. Big mistake.

Youch! I dropped the cord. Jimmy and I stood glaring at each other.

I snarled.

Then Jimmy did something no human had ever done to me before—or since.

He took his end of the cord and whipped it across my back. Hard. I yipped and crouched, ready to spring if he tried it again. It was a standoff. But Jimmy had the upper hand, and we both knew it.

"You wanna live another day? Then earn it!" he snarled back.

Did I want to live another day? You bet. Lots of other days. Long enough to see this guy and his buddies in the slammer. So when he threw the stick at me this time, I caught it. And went into my routine.

Up went the stick, high into the air. Up goes me on my hind legs, catching it. Jimmy throws in the second stick, then a third. I'm juggling!

Out of the corner of my eye, I saw the sandbox kids dragging their moms over. The college kids were ambling our way, too. Even the chess fans were looking up from the board. Got 'em! Kid, I love showbiz. And it loves me back. I felt better already.

I finished up with a flip, then caught the last stick and dropped it next to the tip cup. While the audience was still applauding, I sat up and begged. Cute, huh? The tip cup was overflowing in no time.

"My dog thanks you! And I thank you!" Jimmy said as he took a bow. *My* bow. The tip cup had worked harder than he had.

"Hey—it's the dog with the monkey!" a little voice said from the fountain.

Shocked, I turned. There, taking a bath, was Dolores, the wild lorikeet! She wasn't alone. There were three or four other parrots from the flock splashing around, too.

"Dolores!" I gasped. "What are you doing here?!"

"We fly free, dog. Remember? Where's your monkey?" she asked.

I filled her in as quick as I could. Her friends stopped splashing to listen. Dolores ruffled her feathers angrily.

"We owe you, dog. You freed us from the humming beans' dangly-tangly. Say the word—*Libertad!*—and we'll attack!"

My mind raced. Sure, maybe they could get Jimmy to drop the leash. But wait—where would that leave Baby? I might not be able to find my way back to him.

I'd made a promise to that little pop-eyed pooch. A Le Chien never goes back on his word.

"No! Not yet. This humming bean's got a buddy of mine caged up, too. Do you know where the other park is? The one you took us to when we met?"

Dolores nodded.

"My monkey—I mean, *Rita's* there, hiding up in a tree. Shadow us and see where this guy takes me. Then go and get her. Tonight!"

"Done. Anything else?" Dolores asked.

A scheme was taking shape in my powerful poodle brain. But it would take guts. And luck. And Rita, and . . .

Ha! I had it!

"When you bring Rita, bring El Jefe, too!"

HOW THAT DAY did drag on!

We'd raked in so much dough that Jimmy decided to add a second show. And a third. And a fourth.

Finally, the last passersby had passed by. It was dark in the park.

But Dolores and her friends never budged. When Jimmy was finally ready to head home, they fluttered off the fountain and followed. They had the sense to stay up high, out of sight. Every now and then I could hear them squawk to each other.

When we got back to the apartment building I saw Dolores fly off. A couple of her pals flew up to the top of a lamppost and perched there. A stakeout!

Jimmy led me up the stairs and into the apartment. Gerry was there, reading the newspaper. He didn't even turn around when Jimmy dumped the day's take onto the table.

"Forty-seven bucks and change!" Jimmy crowed. "Tomorrow we'll go to . . ."

Gerry turned around then. His face was a big fat storm cloud.

"There ain't gonna be no tomorrow. Lacie Whyte won't pay!"

What?!

Jimmy looked stunned. He plopped down on the couch and started reading over Gerry's shoulder. I crept closer to peek.

A photo of the glamorous Lacie Whyte was splashed across the front page. She was flipping back her long blond hair. A dozen microphones were in her face. Above her a headline blared, AIRHEAD HEIRESS SAYS "NO" TO RANSOM, OFFERS TEN-THOUSAND-DOLLAR REWARD.

Jimmy pulled off his wig hat and rubbed his head. "Whoa. That stinks."

"*Whoa, that stinks!*" Gerry mocked. "Brilliant, Einstein."

Suddenly the door flew open. We all whirled to see

Quinn slam it closed behind her. Her eyes were practically shooting sparks.

"Have you heard the latest?" she demanded. Then, putting on a high whiny voice that was supposed to sound like Lacie Whyte's, she went on, "Even though I miss Baby, like, sooo much, I'm not gonna pay the ransom. Because that, like, just encourages dognapping." Quinn's shoulders slumped. She dropped the act. "We're dead!"

"I got an idea, Quinn," Jimmy offered. "How about Gerry takes Baby in and claims the reward?"

Quinn shook her head. "How long do you think it would take the cops to connect Gerry to you? And you to me? It's a trap!"

"What do we do?" Gerry asked.

"Do? We ditch that stinkin' Baby, that's what. Unless you want to risk the slammer for a measly ten grand." She turned her burning eyes on me. I shrank back.

"Get rid of that one, too. I don't ever wanna see another dog!"

"How?" Gerry demanded.

"Quietly. Late tonight. So that when you take the bodies out, nobody will see."

Bodies?! Wait a minute. I was still using mine!

"Put him in the back room. I don't like the way he's lookin' at me," Quinn snapped.

I let Jimmy lead me back to the locked bedroom. He shoved me in and closed the door. Baby, who'd been curled up on his blanket, sprang to his feet. One look at my hangdog expression told him there was trouble. His little tail stopped wagging.

"What is it, Pete? What's the mattuh?"

"Well, it's like this. Those guys . . . your owner . . . we . . ."

It's amazing how hard it was to get started. I was fumbling for words, when there was a sudden sharp tap on the window. I dashed over and grabbed the shade in my teeth. I gave it a jerk that brought it clattering to the floor.

Baby took one look, then tumbled down in a faint.

There, pressed against the glass, was Rita's ugly mug!

To Baby, she must have looked like a nightmare. To me, she was a dream come true. In all the fuss, I'd almost forgotten that Dolores had gone after her.

Talk about showing up on cue!

I put my muzzle to the glass so she could hear me. "Rita! Can you open the window?"

Rita frowned. Putting her hands on the outside of

the sash, she strained to lift it. The old window creaked, but didn't budge. Rita stopped pushing. "It must be locked! Should I break it?"

I thought fast. If the bad guys heard glass breaking, they'd come running for sure.

But we couldn't stay here. I looked at Baby, who was coming around. "Rise and shine!" I barked. "I need you on your feet."

Baby lifted his little head and looked at Rita. "Who's that?" he quavered.

"Rita. One of the friends I was telling you about. Here comes another one!"

El Jefe had landed! The Great Dog Rescue was about to commence.

El Jefe rapped sharply on the glass with his beak and croaked, "*Libertad!* Let the freedom fight begin!"

"Rita can't open the window, and we can't risk breaking it. I know how you feel about humming beans. But some of them are good. We need their help. You're the only one who can get them here. Will you?"

El Jefe shifted from one foot to the other. We waited. Finally, he nodded. "The free ones never forget a friend. What do you wish me to do, *amigo*?"

I told him. He listened carefully.

"Can you do it?" I asked.

"*Si.*"

I was just filling Rita in on her part, when, behind us, the door flew open. There stood Gerry and Jimmy, each carrying a gunnysack. They spotted Rita in the window and froze.

Jimmy grabbed Gerry's arm. "Is that a monkey!?"

Gerry stared. Rita waved.

"Naw, it's a chimp. Those things are worth money!" he breathed. "We could sell it and get enough to blow town!"

He edged toward Rita, slowly opening his sack. "I'll grab it. Just open the window, nice and slow."

Both of them put on big phony smiles as they came closer. Rita smiled back.

Jimmy unlocked the window at the top, then slowly slid it open.

Rita didn't move.

I stood there, praying she wouldn't lose her nerve. We needed those precious seconds. Rita watched, as still as a stuffed toy. Gerry's arm snaked out the window. Reaching for her ankle . . .

Quicker than a racing pig, she plunged at him!

Before he could pull back, she slammed the window down on his arm. Gerry squealed. Perfect!

Now, if only El Jefe came through!

He did—with bells on.

From just outside the window, a terrified woman's voice rose in an ear-piercing scream.

"Fire! Help! Fire!"

CHAPTER 21

GET THE DOGS, you idiots!" Quinn had come running at the cry of fire.

But Rita had Gerry's arm in her mighty grip, and wasn't about to let go. Dropping his sack, Jimmy grabbed Gerry and tried to haul him back.

Quinn's eyes lit on Rita. "What *is* that thing?" she demanded.

"A monkey—and it's got Gerry! Help!" Jimmy yelped.

"It can have him." Quinn snatched up the sack and moved toward Baby. "But this one's mine!"

"Watch yourself, Baby!" I yipped.

"She'll nevah take me alive!" Baby snarled back.

Outside, that woman was still screaming. I could hear windows flying open and other people adding their voices to her cries. Somewhere a siren wailed.

Then a man's voice, loud and commanding, came from the fire escape.

"Freeze! Police! We've got you covered!" There went El Jefe again. His old owner must have loved cop shows because he almost fooled me.

Boy, did those humming beans look sick! Rita let loose Gerry's arm, and Gerry and Jimmy put their hands in the air. But Quinn panicked. She dropped the sack and made a break for the front door.

"Come on, Baby! After her!" I barked.

We were right behind her when she ran out into the hall—and practically into the arms of the firemen outside!

"Lady, are you all right? Where's the fire?" one of them asked, grabbing hold of her arm.

Ooh, she was a slick one, that Quinn. "Inside! I'm fine—just let me go!" He did. She made for the stairs.

But she never got there. Forty pounds of flying poodle hit her like a bag of bricks. Another seven pounds of rampaging Chihuahua finished the job. Quinn's head hit the tile floor, hard. She stayed down.

From somewhere inside the apartment, I heard a fireman yelp in surprise. Barreling out of the door came Rita.

"You're okay!" she crowed. She looked at Quinn. "But she's not."

"Rita, meet Baby. Baby, meet Rita. Where's El Jefe?"

"Out on the fire escape, squawking 'Reach for the sky!' That was a stroke of genius, dog. Almost worthy of a chimp. Those two creeps still had their hands in the air when I left to find you."

"It was good, wasn't it?" I paused to bask in the praise.

Just then, the firemen ran out of the apartment. One of them spotted Rita.

"There it is! Dan, radio Animal Control, we got a . . ."

But Dan was gazing past Rita at Baby. Thank goodness he was still wearing that dirty pink sweater.

"Hey—isn't that . . . ?"

The other fireman looked again. His eyebrows zoomed up in surprise.

Dan snapped on his radio. "Captain? You're not gonna believe this. We just found Baby."

CHAPTER 22

THE COPS GOT THERE in time to hear Jimmy babbling a confession as the firemen led him out. Gerry looked kind of green and was holding his arm funny. Quinn Carey opened her eyes, saw a policeman staring down at her, and cracked like a soft-boiled egg. She, Gerry, and Jimmy were taken off in handcuffs, all blaming each other at the tops of their lungs.

A nice lady from Animal Control came up just as they were leaving. She looked at Baby, at me, then at Rita. She whistled.

"That's Baby, all right. And I've got a 'missing' poster on that chimp up at the office. The one that circus lost in the storm? In fact, the poodle could be . . ." She stared at me, frowning.

I didn't need a mirror to tell me I looked more like a stray than a star. To introduce myself, I threw a couple of flips.

She laughed. "Yup, that'd be their star dog. Who'd have believed it? How'd you two get all the way to St. Louis?"

She squatted down and held her arms out to Rita. Rita let herself be carried off like a tired toddler. The lady's partner put Baby in a dog carrier and me on a leash.

We spent the night in comfortable quarters at the animal shelter.

It didn't take long for the Animal Control lady to track down Circus Martinez. Greta and Mike were there to get us first thing the next morning. Did I lick their faces? Boy, did I! Rita hopped up and down like a pogo stick, chittering with joy.

"Pete! Oh, my goodness!" gasped Greta. "We were worried sick!"

"Good old Rita!" Mike said, hugging her next. "What an adventure. If only they could talk!"

If only!

Suddenly, in swept Lacie Whyte, bodyguards trailing. She looked around the dreary shelter. Her pretty face crumpled. "I'm Lacie Whyte. You have my dog?"

When the Animal Control lady hurried in with Baby and set him on the floor, Lacie stared in horror. Bedraggled, Baby blinked back at her. With a sob, Lacie swept him up in her arms. She rained kisses on his ugly little mug. "Oh, Baby!" she cooed. "Widdie biddums!"

"*Awk!* What's she doing?" Baby wheezed, taken aback.

"Those are people kisses, dog. I think she missed you!" I yipped.

It was like the sun suddenly shone on his face. "She likes me! She willy, willy likes me!" he panted.

Half an hour later, we were all on the steps of the shelter fielding questions from the press. Greta held Rita's hand. I leaned my head against Mike's leg. The cameras were flashing, mostly at Lacie Whyte. Baby was snuggled up in her arms, wearing a clean sweater. He looked like a dog who knows he's loved.

"I just wanted to thank everyone for all of your help

and stuff during this whole yucky thing," Lacie was saying. "I have no clue how they, like, did it? But these two circus animals found Baby. So they're, like, getting the reward."

Mike and Greta looked at each other, thrilled. I was happy, too. But money doesn't mean much to animals. What counts to us is loyalty.

And I had some unfinished business with a certain lopsided duck.

Now the reporters were peppering Mike and Greta with questions. For the moment, nobody was watching me. I got up and started off.

I was all the way down the steps and on the sidewalk before Mike noticed I was leaving.

"Pete? Pete? Here, boy!" He whistled.

Ordinarily, I do what Mike tells me. But I was a dog on a mission. I knew he'd figure it out. For humans, Mike and Greta are pretty bright.

Rita pulled loose from Greta's hand and caught up to me. "You know the way?"

"We passed it coming here last night," I told her. "I saw it from the van. And I can smell the river."

Good thing Mike and Greta were in shape. It was a brisk half mile to the park where we'd left Quackers and we couldn't risk losing them. Rita was having her usual effect on humans. Which is, to send them screaming in the opposite direction. I knew Mike and Greta would explain and calm everyone down. We just had to get to Quackers before they caught up.

When I hit the park, I made for the pond. There he was, sailing around with the local ducks. Quackers spotted me and broke into mad squawks of joy. He waded out, wings flapping. "You're alive! You came back!"

"Well, sure. We circus folk have to stick together." I grinned.

His chest puffed out with pride.

Mike and Greta came huffing into the park and spotted us. The reporters were hard on their heels and caught the second act of our reunion live on camera.

"Oh, Pete!" Greta said, hugging me. "No more running off! We can't do without our star attraction!"

Star attraction? Music to my doggy ears, kid.

"Who's this?" Mike asked.

Rita threw her arms around Quackers. He snuggled his head into her neck. I sat next to them and wagged my tail. We made as cute a family picture as you ever saw. Considering Rita was in it, I mean.

Mike and Greta stared at us, then at each other.
Sometimes it takes a while for humans to catch on.
Even the well-trained ones.

"Pete and Rita made friends with a duck?" Mike
asked.

"Mike, I think they want the duck to come home
with us."

Rita grinned and squeezed Quackers until he
squeaked. I barked and danced around on my hind legs.

Suddenly, a familiar croak sounded from the tree above us.

"*Amigos!* Are these humming beans pestering you? Say the word and we'll attack!" A raucous chorus of chirps, caws, and whistles sounded from all over the park. It was El Jefe and the gang!

"No! Don't attack! They're our friends!" I yipped. Rita jumped into Mike's arms and gave him a noisy kiss on the cheek. The poor guy nearly keeled over. Chimp breath is no bunch of violets.

"They're here to take us home," I barked up at the tree.

"Ah! This is good, eh?" El Jefe called.

"Better than good!" I agreed. "But thank you—for everything. If you ever want to go into show business, get in touch. You could have your own act!"

"Showbiz is not for the birds. For us there is only— *Libertad!*" With that, he rose into the sky, his flock of feathered freedom fighters behind him. "Fly safe, *amigos*! May we meet again!"

That very afternoon, me and Rita, our humans, and a duck hopped a plane to Sarasota.

CHAPTER 23

T HE PUBLICITY had beat us home. The ringmaster was so delighted with the free press, he forgot
all about our little tangle in the ring. He was there to
meet us when we got off the plane. He kneeled down
and embraced me. Gee—was that a tear in his eye?

"We thought you two were goners!" he crowed, pat-
ting my head. "It's a miracle, Mike." He honked his
nose into his damp red hanky. "You know what we're
gonna do? We're gonna put on a show! We'll do a final
performance, before we shut down for the winter. And
we'll double the ticket prices! No—triple 'em!"

Mike took us to the animal barn, so we could chow
down with the others. I knew they'd be happy to see
Rita. But what about me? What about the Silent

Treatment? Would I go back to being an outcast? Alone and unloved?

PeeWee, the ostrich, was the first to catch sight of us. Those golf-ball eyes nearly popped out of his head.

"They're back!" he squawked. Everyone's head jerked up from their feed. Suddenly, the air was full of neighs, roars, and yips. Were they happy to see me? If they'd been any happier, I'd have been trampled.

"You're supposed to be dead!" PeeWee said.

I was trying to think of a snappy comeback when every member of the Performing Pups leaped on me at once. My tail was wagging so hard I thought it might come unscrewed.

"Darlings!" It was Imelda Lipizzaner. She nuzzled Rita, then me. Her sisters did, too. I licked Sophie's velvety nose.

"Where have you guys been?" Zamba, the tiger, demanded.

"Everywhere and back." Rita grinned.

"Am I dreaming?" Lucky yawned. "So you guys made up? You're partners again?"

That was my cue. I nudged Quackers out from behind Rita. "You bet we're partners. Only now, we're a trio. Guys, gals—meet our brave and talented buddy, Quackers."

Our fellow cast members looked taken aback.

"Ah—a duck?" Sophie Lipizzaner asked.

Rita stepped in. "Not just any duck, Sophie. A duck with skills. A duck with heart. A duck with . . . star quality."

There was a moment's silence.

Zamba spoke up.

"But . . . a duck?" he rumbled. "And an

amateur? Not to insult your buddy, but I never heard of a duck in the circus."

Quackers, suddenly shy, stuck his head under his wing. Rita looked defiantly around at the doubting faces.

"He dances, he does impressions. He saved our hides about half a dozen times," she said. "If circus is loyalty, if circus is family, this kid is circus."

I jumped in. "And Rita and I won't go on without him. Period."

Rita and I held our breaths. The animals looked at each other. Then, Czarina stepped forward and bent her long neck down to Quackers. He pulled his head out from under his wing and blinked at her. She smiled.

"Hello, Quackers. Vhelcome home."

We'd promised Quackers a place in the circus. But doing what? The show was less than two days away! Of course, Mike and Greta couldn't know about it until it happened. So whatever Quackers did, it had to wow 'em. Otherwise, his debut would be his swan song.

"Nobody can learn a routine that fast," I worried. "Maybe he could do some water ballet in the kiddie pool?"

"How's that gonna wow 'em? Everybody's seen a duck swim."

"Hey, what about my impressions?" Quackers asked.

"Not yet," I said. "The world isn't ready."

Suddenly Rita brightened up and snapped her fingers. "Got it!"

"Got what?" I said. But she was already loping away.

Moments later, she was back, pushing the clowns' toy baby carriage. "Here you go, partner. Hop in!" she crowed.

Quackers blinked at the baby carriage, his beak hanging open. "What do you call that thing?"

"This? This is what we call a, uh . . . a star vehicle!" Rita said. She was careful not to catch my eye. "You, Quackers, are going to make your entrance in it at the sold-out, one-performance-only Welcome Home Circus Spectacular!"

Quackers turned to me. "Pete? You really think I'm ready for the big time?"

"Listen to me, duck. I've been in this game my whole life. I know what it takes. Do you trust me?"

He nodded.

"Well, good—because you're going out into that ring a farm animal. But you're coming back a star!"

CHAPTER 24

THE **CIRCUS** was in a flurry, getting ready for the big night. Time rushed by in a blur. As Quacker's debut drew closer, I wondered if we'd all wind up with egg on our faces. Would he take to the spotlight like a duck to water? Or would he chicken out?

Before we knew it, it was showtime.

Since "Pete and Rita" was the big draw, the ring-master had put us back in the headline spot at the end of the first act. We did our routine with the usual snap and dazzle, and the audience was eating it up. But when I leaped down off of the rolla-bolla ball and ran into the wings, I could tell they didn't know what to expect.

Tah-dahhhh! Out I trotted, pushing the baby carriage with Quackers in it. I could hear some surprised murmurs from the bleachers. A duck? The program hadn't said anything about a duck!

Quackers' baby bonnet was cockeyed. There was a crazy, spooked glint in his eye. I knew that look. Stage fright! He was flapping his wings like he was gonna make a break for it. Rita, dancing along beside us, shot me a worried glance.

We must have looked awfully cute, because the applause started to build as we passed.

Quackers heard it, too. And just like that, the stage fright disappeared. He stared around at all the smiling faces like a duck in a dream.

"Quackers! Don't just sit there! Go into your number!" I barked.

He hopped out of the carriage. "Now?!"

"Now!" Rita grinned.

And Quackers danced.

He leaped, he reeled, he flapped. The band struck up "The Blue Danube," and feathers flew. Rita and I stood back and let him have the spotlight. When he was too pooped to prance, he jumped back into the baby carriage. Rita took him for a victory lap around the ring.

Wow! Did the crowd go nuts? Pal, they went peanuts, walnuts, hazelnuts—every kind of nuts! Quackers stuck his head out and nodded this way and that. Rita and I took our bows. I could see the other animals in the wings, adding their noise to the crowd's roar. It was a night to remember. The kind that only happens in storybooks—unless you're lucky enough to be in the circus, like us.

Rita shoved a sharp elbow in my ribs. "Hey! Did you see who's sitting ringside?"

I'd been so caught up in the show that I hadn't checked out the audience. I looked.

There was Lacie Whyte—and Baby!

Rita and I ran over to them. Baby put his little paws on the rail.

"You guys are gweat!" he yapped. "I had no idea!" Lacie had bought him a nice new sweater. Blue. "We flew in on the pwivate jet just to supwise you."

"We're surprised!" Rita said. "Who's the lady?"

Lacie's bodyguard was holding a cute little Chihuahua in a pink sweater. She waved a dainty paw at us.

"Lacie was so glad to have me back she bought me a fwiend. Say hello, Pilah!"

"I've heard so much about you!" Pilar yipped, wagging her stump of a tail.

"Did you see me?" Quackers asked happily. "Did you catch my act?"

Lacie was beaming at us all. "Oh wow, like, look at them? Is that the sweetest? It's like they actually know each other!" And she flipped her long blond hair, right into her cotton candy.

Rita grinned at me. "So, the Airhead Heiress has a heart after all."

I grinned back. "Sometimes you've got to lose a thing, to find out how much it means to you."

"So true, Partner."

There really *is* no place like home.

"Now," Rita said, "let's get this duck backstage before he starts doing impressions."

By the end of the winter layoff, you'd have thought Quackers was hatched in the center ring. Man, that duck can really ride a rolla-bolla ball! Those flat feet fairly fly.

Come see for yourself, next time we roll through your town. We're easy to find. Just follow the crowds. Grab some pink popcorn on your way in.

And sit up close. You won't want to miss a thing.